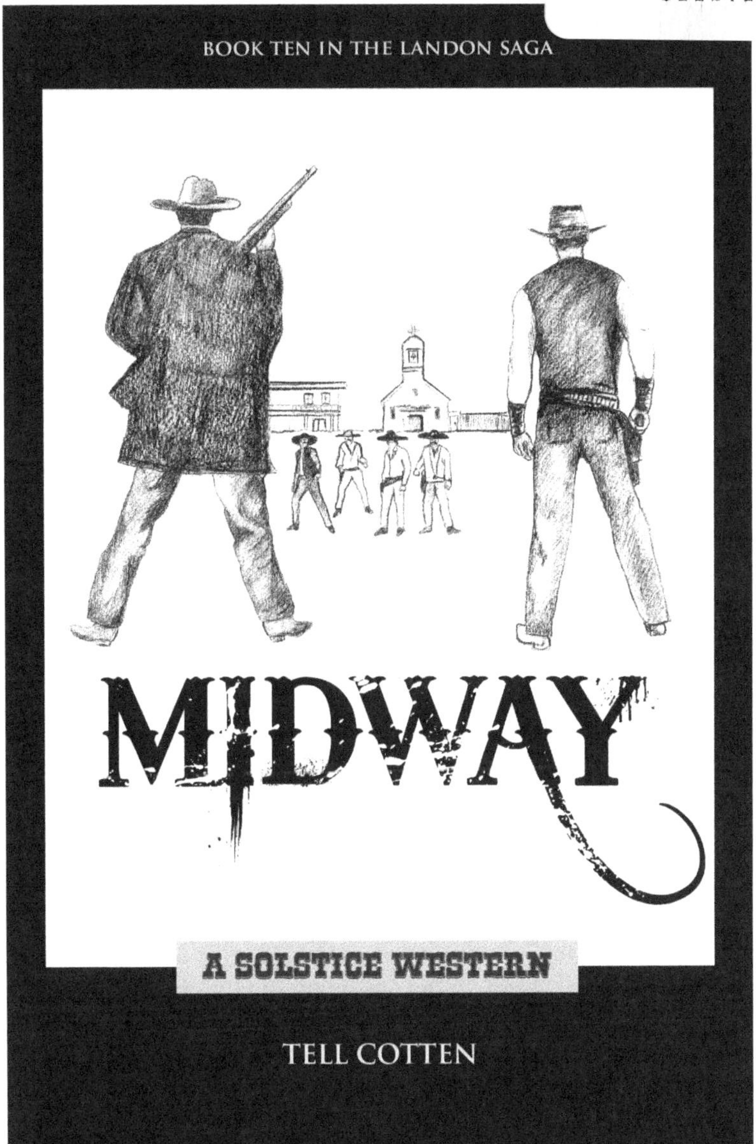
BOOK TEN IN THE LANDON SAGA
MIDWAY
A SOLSTICE WESTERN
TELL COTTEN

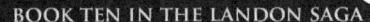

MIDWAY

Tell Cotten

Dedication
To my mother, Jan Cotten; thanks for the proofreads!

ALL RIGHTS RESERVED

No part of this book may be reproduced or transmitted in any form or by any means, electronic or mechanical, including photocopying, recording, or by any information storage and retrieval system, without permission in writing from the author, except in the case of brief quotations embodied in reviews.

Illustrator: Bill Olivas
www.billolivas.com
wbolivas@yahoo.com

Cover Art:
Marcy Meinke/Converse Printing & Design
www.ConversePrinting.com
mike@converseprinting.com

Publisher's Note:

This is a work of fiction. All names, characters, places, and events are the work of the author's imagination.

Any resemblance to real persons, places, or events is coincidental.

Solstice Publishing - www.solsticepublishing.com

Copyright 2017 Tell Cotten

The Landon Saga currently has five main characters that interact through the novels. For a quick reminder, below is the recent status of each main character.

Rondo Landon: Is married to Rachel, Mr. Tomlin's daughter. Rondo is an ex-outlaw and lawman. As described in FASTEST GUN AROUND, Rondo agreed to return to Empty-lake and accept the sheriff's job. However, folks at Midway are not aware of this yet.

Yancy Landon: Cousin to Rondo. Newly appointed as a Texas Ranger, and is romantically involved with Jessica Tussle, who is J.T. Tussle's niece.

Cooper Landon: Cousin to Rondo, and Yancy's older brother. Married to Josie, and has an adopted son, Wyatt, who was rescued from the Apaches. Like Yancy, he is also a newly appointed Texas Ranger.

Lee Mattingly: An ex-outlaw, and a friend of Rondo's. Romantically involved with April Gibson. He also owns part interest in The Palace Hotel, along with partner Brian Clark.

August 'Winchester' Landon: A cousin to Yancy, Cooper, and Rondo. Winchester is currently an Apache scout in the New Mexico Territory.

Part One
"The Day Before"

CHAPTER ONE

I knew something was amiss when I saw Yancy's face.

He was *smiling*.

Yancy Landon is my younger brother. He has a smaller build than me, spry, and is in good shape.

Most of the time, he's a very somber person. He never talks unless he has to, and when he does he's clear, certain, and to the point. He's also painfully honest, no matter the cost.

My brother is well known for his skills with his Colt six-shooter. He also has a natural knack for finding trouble.

I'll be the first to admit I'm not as good with a six-shooter. My specialty is with my Henry rifle. I'm real accurate with it, and mighty quick too. I have a special way of swinging it up, and it's almost as fast as Yancy's draw.

My name is Cooper Landon.

Folks best describe me as tall, wide-shouldered, and rawboned. Whenever possible, I'm more relaxed than Yancy. I like life to go at a slow pace, and I also like to think things out before I act.

Yancy and I were newly appointed Texas Rangers. We mainly worked alone, and we answered to Judge Parker himself.

We were on our way home to Midway, Texas. I was anxious, because I hadn't seen my wife, Josie, or adopted son, Wyatt, in a while.

These past few weeks we'd been in the New Mexico Territory, helping our cousin, Rondo, rescue his wife from Apaches. It had been a dangerous task, but the conflict ended with satisfactory results.

We were now about an hour away from J.T. Tussle's headquarters. The countryside was mostly open, with a few rolling hills, and some mesquite bushes and catclaw spread about.

I was eager to reach town, but Yancy insisted we stop at Tussle's headquarters. He didn't say it, but I knew he wanted to see Jessica, so I didn't object much.

I figured Wyatt might be there anyway. Tussle had given him a summer job, and Wyatt spent every available moment at Tussle's ranch. He hardly ever came home, and that worried Josie.

I wasn't as concerned. Wyatt was growing up, and I figured it was only natural for a boy to spread his wings some.

We trotted north in an easy trot. Jug-head, our loyal but stubborn pack mule, trailed along behind me.

Yancy was still smiling like a fool. It was irritating for some reason, so I cleared my throat.

"What is it," I said, interrupting his thoughts of bliss.

Yancy blinked, turned in the saddle, and looked at me. "What?"

"That thing on your face," I explained.

"What thing?"

"Your outer lips are pointed upwards," I said. "You know; opposite of a frown."

"Was I smiling?" Yancy looked sheepish.

"Shocking, I know. But yes, you were."

"No law against it," Yancy defended.

"No, but you could have warned me," I replied. "When you change I get worried."

"I reckon I'm just eager."

"Thinking about Jessica?" I smiled knowingly.

Yancy nodded. If he was embarrassed, he didn't show it.

"You remember what I planned on doing when we got back home?" He asked.

"Something about marriage," I recalled.

"That's right," Yancy said, and declared, "I'm going to ask her."

"Good for you," I replied, then asked, "When?"

"I don't know. Soon as we get there, I guess."

8

I was startled.

"Today?"

"Sure. Why not?"

"Look at us," I objected. "We've been traveling for weeks. I don't even remember the last bath we've had. I can smell the sweat on you, and you're downwind."

"Aw, it ain't *that* bad," Yancy sniffed the air.

"You're missing the point," I tried again. "A woman likes to be romanced a little. Swept off her feet, not knocked off by some sour, stenchy breeze."

"You saying I should take a bath?"

"I would strongly suggest it."

Yancy scrunched his face in thought.

"There's a dirt tank ahead," he recalled. "We could stop there."

"Be better than nothing," I replied.

Yancy nodded and turned his horse toward the lakebed. Jug-head and I followed after him.

"How 'bout you?" Yancy asked.

I considered it and shook my head.

"Naw, I'll wait until town."

Yancy looked at me and raised an eyebrow.

"What about the sour odor?"

I shrugged and said, "I'm already married."

"I should tell Josie you said that," Yancy replied, and we both chuckled.

CHAPTER TWO

The water was brown and murky by the time Yancy finished his bath.

"Did you stir that tank up, or did *all* that come off you?" I asked while Yancy dried off.

He glanced at the water.

"Probably a little of both," he suggested, and I grinned in agreement.

Yancy crawled back into his clothes. Next, he took off an old bandage and re-bandaged his minor wound.

Yancy was real proud of his injury. He had received a gash on his forearm while fighting with an Apache, and each time we discussed the fight it got more and more glorious.

"How's the arm?" I asked.

"Fine," Yancy replied as he stepped into the saddle. "Not even bleeding anymore."

"Then why the bandage?"

A sheepish look crossed Yancy's face, and I sighed and shook my head.

"Pathetic," I said softly.

"What?" Yancy frowned at me.

"You want sympathy from Jessica," I accused.

Yancy started to deny it, but then grinned.

"I've been wearing this bandage for weeks," he said. "Few more days won't hurt."

"It's *your* conscience, not mine," I said, and we nudged our horses forward.

"How do I look?" Yancy asked.

"Not much different," I replied. "But, at least you *smell* better."

"I could use a shave," Yancy mused.

"*And* cleaner clothes," I added.

"Well, a feller can't have *everything*."

"Mebbe Jessica will be so overjoyed to see you, she won't notice your rough appearance," I said.

"You think so?"

"Not really. I was just trying to be helpful."

Yancy scowled at me, and we said no more.

CHAPTER THREE

We finally spotted Tussle's headquarters from afar. The houses and corrals merged together into one form, but they spread out as we got closer.

It was an impressive layout.

The main house was huge, multi-roomed, and had numerous windows that opened up to the spacious front porch.

Across from the main house was the cookhouse and a large bunkhouse, and beyond that was a barn, a set of corrals, a saddle house, and some storage sheds.

We rode up beside the barn and spotted a few cowhands. They were at the corrals, working with some broncs.

"Tussle hired some new hands," Yancy noted.

"Looks like," I replied.

A tall, muscular cowpuncher was in the middle of a bronc ride, and we watched in silent admiration.

The horse could really buck. He took huge, twisting jumps, and he sucked backwards each time he was in the air. However, the cowpuncher stuck with him, and round and round they went.

"That's a mighty big fella," Yancy observed.

"Big as a mountain," I agreed.

"Most bronc riders are small."

"He's not," I replied.

Yancy nodded, and his face turned wistful.

"I never could ride a bucking horse," he lamented, then added, "And I *am* small."

"Or bucking mules," I reminded, and I smiled when I felt Yancy's glare.

I looked over to where the other cowpunchers had gathered. As I had suspected, I spotted Wyatt sitting on the top rail.

He had grown some. His face was covered with sandy looking freckles, and he had dark hair.

His face was flushed with excitement, and I grinned as I watched him. After a moment, I turned my attention back to the bronc ride.

The horse took an abrupt spin that the cowpuncher wasn't expecting. He was thrown forward, and he went flying through the air and landed on his back with a thump.

Yancy and I grimaced.

"That had to hurt," Yancy commented.

"Imagine it did," I agreed.

To our surprise, the muscled cowpuncher laughed good-naturedly. He jumped to his feet, dusted himself off, and looked over at Wyatt and grinned.

"Thought I had him," we heard him say, and the other cowpunchers laughed and gave him a hard time.

"Tough too," Yancy said admiringly.

"Naw, he's just younger," I replied.

"We ain't *that* old," Yancy objected.

"We aren't," I agreed. "But, we ain't *that* young either."

Yancy snorted in response.

The muscled cowpuncher caught the horse and led him to the middle of the corral. I expected him to get back on, but instead he looked at Wyatt.

"Want to try him, boss?" We heard him say.

I was surprised by the offer, and I uttered a disgruntled grunt.

"No, he sure doesn't!" I snorted.

Wyatt had other ideas. He nodded eagerly, jumped off the fence, and approached the horse.

I scowled and started to dismount, but Yancy stopped me.

"Don't do it," he warned.

"What?" I glared at him.

"Wyatt's growing up, Coop. It'll embarrass him if you make a scene."

"He has no business riding that horse," I retorted.

"Mebbe not, but it's too late now."

I looked back just in time to see Wyatt grab the reins, put a foot in the stirrup, and swing on.

"Lord, have mercy," I prayed softly.

CHAPTER FOUR

The muscular cowpuncher held the horse by the reins while Wyatt got settled in the saddle.

"You ready, boss?" He asked.

Wyatt nodded and ducked his head.

The cowpuncher turned loose, stepped back, and said, "He's all yours!"

The bronc didn't realize he was free. He just stood there until Wyatt nudged him with his spurs.

The horse exploded, and Wyatt's head snapped back. He took a huge jump and landed hard, but Wyatt stayed with him.

"Use your spurs!" The muscular cowpuncher yelled encouragement.

"Quit milking the saddle horn!" Another yelled.

Round and round they went. The horse took big, twisting jumps, and I could hear the saddle leathers pop each time he landed.

Wyatt stayed in the saddle as if he belonged, and he was gaining confidence with each jump.

"He's gonna stick!" Yancy yelled enthusiastically.

As soon as Yancy spoke, the horse sucked backwards. It took Wyatt by surprise, and he went flying forward. He hit the top rail of the corral, bounced, and landed in a heap on the other side.

The dust settled slowly, and Wyatt made abrupt, jerky movements. I figured the air had been knocked out of him, and I knew all too well how that felt.

I leaped off my horse and ran toward him. He tried to sit up, but then groaned and went back down.

A few seconds passed, and Wyatt squeaked out a loud, painful sucking sound. To my relief, he started gasping air into his lungs right as I reached him. I squatted beside him, and Yancy and the cowpunchers came up behind me.

"Wyatt!" I said. "You dying?"

He shook his head, closed his eyes, made a moaning sound, and inhaled deeply.

There was nothing to do but wait it out. Wyatt huffed and puffed, but finally his breathing slowed. He opened his eyes, blinked several times, and looked at me with a dazed expression.

"What are you doing here," he muttered.

"We just rode in," I replied. "Are you all right?"

Wyatt suddenly realized he'd been bucked off. He scowled and looked embarrassed.

"I'll live," he replied.

"Is anything broke?"

"I said I'm fine."

He struggled to his feet, and I grabbed him underneath his arm and helped.

"You almost had him, boss!" The muscular cowpuncher said.

"I will next time," Wyatt muttered.

Before the cowpuncher could reply, I looked at him and scowled my displeasure.

I must have looked upset. The cowpuncher grinned sheepishly, nodded, and climbed back into the corral. The other cowpunchers went with him, and I glanced at Yancy.

He smiled knowingly. He walked over to the horses, leaving me alone with Wyatt.

I looked back at Wyatt. He was dusting himself off, and he displayed a scowl on his face.

I coughed and cleared my throat.

"We should talk," I said.

CHAPTER FIVE

Wyatt looked at me a moment and nodded.

"I reckon we should," he said, and his voice was surprisingly deep.

I suddenly realized something, and my mouth fell open.

"You're talking!" I exclaimed.

"Sure," Wyatt shrugged.

"When did this happen?" I asked, pleased.

"A while back," Wyatt replied. "Tussle thought it might be a good idea, so I said I would."

"That's all he said?"

"Sure."

I thought of the countless hours Josie and I had spent, trying everything we could think of to make Wyatt speak. I almost mentioned it, but decided not to.

"Does Josie know?" I asked instead.

"Sure."

'Sure' seemed to be Wyatt's favorite word. I frowned at that, but let it go.

"What were you doing on that horse?" I changed the subject, and I tried to sound stern.

"I was *trying* to ride him."

"You could have been killed," I objected.

"It happens."

"Doesn't that scare you, at least a little?"

"I like to be scared," Wyatt declared. "It feels good."

"It does?" I raised an eyebrow, and then tried another angle. "Don't you think you're a little young to be riding broncs?"

"Rondo rode broncs when he was my age," Wyatt reminded. "You told me so yourself."

"But he was really good at it," I said, and then winced at how that sounded.

An irked expression crossed Wyatt's face.

"I'm good at it too," he said defiantly. "Tex says I'm a natural."

"Who's Tex?" I asked.

Wyatt pointed at the muscular cowpuncher, and I narrowed my eyes at him.

"So that's Tex," I commented, then asked, "Why does he call you boss?"

"Tex calls everybody that," Wyatt shrugged. "'Course, Tex ain't his real name neither. That's just what everybody calls *him*."

"Isn't," I corrected, then added, "I should meet Tex."

Excitement filled Wyatt's face.

"You'd like him. He's a *real* cowpuncher."

"You don't say."

"He's worked for all the main outfits," Wyatt continued. "He can really ride a horse too!"

"I noticed," I said, and then I looked back at Wyatt. "But that's Tex's job. It's not yours."

"It is now," Wyatt declared with pride. "Tussle gave me a raise last month, and he told Tex to teach me all he knows about horses."

"Is that right," I said softly.

"Sure."

"Tussle had no right to do that," I objected. "He should have talked to me first."

"You weren't around. In fact, you're never around."

I didn't have an answer for that, so I didn't attempt one.

"I'm glad we have a moment to talk," Wyatt took advantage of the silence. "There's something I'd like to discuss."

"And what's that?" I was curious.

"It's about Josie."

"What about her?"

Wyatt paused while he searched for the right words.

"I appreciate you and Josie taking me in," he finally said. "But, you're not my real parents. They're dead."

His words stung a little, but I tried hard not to show it.

"I know that," I said.

"I'm thirteen years old," Wyatt reminded. "It's time for me to find my own way."

"Mind explaining that a little?" I frowned.

"My parents raised me right," Wyatt replied. "I know what I'm doing, and I can make my own choices now."

"Is that right."

"Yes, sir."

Even though I disagreed, I was proud of him for saying so.

"Your parents did a good job," I acknowledged.

"I know Josie wants children," Wyatt continued. "But, I'm not it."

I had no reply for that, so I just nodded.

"But don't think I'm not grateful," Wyatt added. "I'll never forget what you did for me. You and Yancy saved my life."

"Once you start talking, you don't stop," I jested.

"I just want you to know that I appreciate everything," he replied.

"I understand, I think."

Wyatt nodded, and it was silent a moment.

"You might talk to Josie," I suggested. "You know how she feels about you."

"I'll talk to her tonight," he replied. "We're riding into town anyways."

"We?" I narrowed my eyes.

"Me and Tex, and some of the boys."

"I see."

"I'll come by."

"Want to eat supper?" I offered.

It was no secret my wife wasn't a very good cook, and Wyatt shifted his feet uncomfortably.

"How 'bout *after* supper?" He asked.

I tried not to smile.

19

"That'll be fine," I said.

Wyatt grinned.

"I'll be there," he promised, then added, "Well, I'd best get back to work."

I nodded, and Wyatt turned toward the corrals. He took one step but then stopped.

"Thanks for understanding," he said.

He looked back at me, and several seconds passed.

"I'm trying," I finally said.

I was surprised when he turned abruptly towards me and extended his hand. We shook, and I couldn't help but notice how firm his grip was.

"See you tonight," he said.

For some reason, I couldn't reply. I just nodded and tried to smile.

Wyatt released my hand. He grinned, spun around, and climbed back into the corrals.

As I watched him go, I felt I had just lost something I'd never get back.

CHAPTER SIX

I walked over to Yancy, but my thoughts were still on Wyatt. It had been a surprising exchange of words, and I didn't know what to think.

Yancy must have known how I felt, because he shot me a sympathetic look.

"Want to talk about it?" He offered.

"No," I said shortly.

"Might help."

I looked at Yancy and frowned.

"You remember when you said talk was overrated?"

Yancy thought a moment.

"No, but it sounds like me."

"This is one of those times."

"Understood," Yancy smiled faintly. A few seconds passed, and he added, "Still, I couldn't help but overhear some of your conversation."

"I'm sure you were straining your ears," I said sourly.

"Like I said; he's growing up."

"Yeah," I grunted. "He's thirteen years old and thinks he knows everything."

"So did we, at his age."

I snorted in response, and the conversation ended.

Yancy handed me the reins to my horse, and we walked up to the main house. There was a hitching rail close by, and we tied our horses and Jug-head to it.

My face was mulish, but Yancy looked excited as we stepped up onto the porch and approached the front door.

"They replaced the window," Yancy gestured.

A bullet had shattered the front window during a raid not that long ago, and I nodded as I looked at it.

"Tussle's been busy," I said.

Yancy nodded his agreement. He knocked on the front door, and seconds later we heard footsteps.

The door opened, and Yancy's expression of joy faded when J.T. Tussle appeared in the doorway.

Tussle was a tall man with a wide frame. He had a weathered face that was trenched with deep lines, and those lines changed shape when he smiled or frowned.

He was an ex-rebel, and proud of it. He respected us, but he never forgot that we had fought on different sides.

There were no greetings or pleasantries exchanged. Instead, Tussle just stood there and glared at us.

"What are you two doing here," he grumbled.

Yancy didn't reply. Instead, like he always did, he looked at me, and I sighed and cleared my throat.

"We were riding by, and thought we'd drop in and say hello," I said pleasantly.

Tussle showed no reaction.

"Where's Rondo?" He asked.

"He's at Empty-lake," I replied.

Tussle grunted his displeasure.

"He was supposed to ride down there, pick up his wife, and be right back."

"We ran into trouble," I explained.

"What sort of trouble?"

"Apaches kidnapped his wife."

Tussle's rough appearance softened.

"Rachel?"

"Only wife he has," I replied.

"She all right?" He sounded anxious.

"Everyone's fine," I reassured, then added, "Except for Jeremiah Wisdom, that is."

"Who's that?"

"Feller that was with us. He took a bullet in the gut."

Tussle nodded, and it was silent as he thought on that.

He was very fond of Rondo and Rachel. And, while he would never admit it, I could tell he was relieved to know they were all right.

Tussle glanced at Yancy and changed the subject.

"You ain't here just to say hello," he said bluntly.

"We aren't?" I was surprised.

Tussle pointed a finger at Yancy.

"*You're* here to see Jessica."

His statement was directed at Yancy. I glanced at him for a reply, and several awkward seconds passed before Yancy realized that.

Yancy looked flustered. Finally, he frowned with determination, swallowed, and looked Tussle in the eye.

"I am," he declared.

Tussle grunted. He studied Yancy a moment, and then turned abruptly and disappeared inside.

Yancy was unsure what to do. He glanced at me for help, but I shrugged, passing the decision back to him.

Yancy pursed his lips. He thought a moment, and he took off his hat and stepped inside.

I chuckled softly, removed my hat, and followed after him.

CHAPTER SEVEN

We hadn't been indoors for weeks, so it felt odd to have a roof over us. We paused while our eyes adjusted, and then we waited in the sitting room.

There was a white, fluffy looking chair in the corner. I sat in it, leaned back, sighed, and relaxed.

It was then that the thought of getting the chair dirty occurred to me. I considered getting up, but then shrugged. At the moment, I was just too comfortable to care.

Yancy, however, looked awkward. He sat on the edge of his chair, and he held his hat with both hands. His knuckles were white, and he bent his hat brim back and forth.

I forgot about my own troubles as I watched him.

"Creasing your hat?" I gestured.

Yancy looked at his hands and frowned.

"Just nervous," he admitted.

"Relax," I instructed. "Take deep breaths, and loosen your shoulders."

"That's what you say when you're teaching somebody to shoot," Yancy pointed out.

"When dealing with Jessica, the same concept works," I replied.

Yancy scowled at me. I smiled back, and after that we waited in silence.

The minutes passed slowly. Then there was a rustling of skirts, and Jessica hurried into the room. Tussle was behind her, and he sat in a chair close to the door.

Jessica was in her early twenties. She had a good figure, long blond hair, and light blue eyes. And, as we had already found out, she also had a very feisty side.

Her face was tense. She appeared to be just as nervous as Yancy, maybe even more.

This should be entertaining, I thought.

Nobody spoke. They just stared at each other, and the silence was uncomfortable.

It was one of the most intense looks I had ever seen. An elephant could have been in the room, and neither one would have noticed.

I cleared my throat, hoping to get their attention, but neither one acknowledged me.

Somebody needed to say *something*, so I looked at Tussle and tried to look pleasant.

"Country looked a little dry riding in," I commented.

Tussle seemed disturbed by the distraction. He took his eyes off them and looked at me.

"It is," he said abruptly.

"Had any rain while we've been gone?" I asked, keeping the conversation going.

"Not much."

"Well, mebbe we'll get some soon."

"We'd better," Tussle grunted. "Grass is running out, and in more ways than one."

I didn't understand that last remark, but Tussle was in no mood to explain. I nodded my reply, and the conversation played out.

The room went painfully silent, but then Jessica cleared her throat.

"You're back," she said, her voice strained.

"Said I would," Yancy replied in his normal, non-gentle way.

"You were gone so long," Jessica said. "We were worried."

"Something came up, but it's all tended to now."

Jessica nodded, and nobody spoke. The awkward silence returned, and I just couldn't take it anymore.

"Cows calving yet?" I glanced at Tussle.

Tussle looked at me and frowned his irritation.

"No, they won't start calving for another month."

"Good, good," I said, searching for words. I didn't find any, so the conversation died.

We looked back at Yancy and Jessica. Yancy was reshaping his hat again, and Jessica was gathering her thoughts.

"Will you be here long?" Jessica managed to say.

"No, we just dropped in to say hello. Be dark soon anyway," Yancy replied.

Jessica frowned.

"I meant how long will you be in town?"

"Oh," Yancy looked slightly embarrassed. "No plans to leave, unless something comes up. Got a few things to tend to around here."

"Like what?"

"Well," Yancy took in a big breath and exhaled. "Was hoping to talk to you."

"You were? About what?"

It must have been the enthusiasm of the moment, for Yancy definitely started blubbering.

"You know how I feel–," he paused, then added, "'Bout you."

"Actually, you've never told me."

"Well, I'll say it now," Yancy declared. "I have strong feelings for you, and I'd like us to be married."

Complete shock showed in Jessica's face, and even Tussle was stunned.

"Marriage?"

"Yes, ma'am."

"Is this a proposal?"

"It is," Yancy confirmed, and he looked at Tussle. "With your permission, of course."

Tussle crossed his arms and grunted loudly.

Yancy must have taken that as a 'yes' because he nodded his appreciation and looked back at Jessica.

"Well?"

A pleased and excited look crossed her face, but then she tried to look stern. She placed her hands on her hips and stomped her foot.

"You stay gone for months, and then you show up all unannounced and expect me to marry you?"

"I was hoping you would."

"Well!" Jessica declared, then grinned. "I accept."

"You do?" Yancy looked surprised.

"Of course I do!"

Yancy grinned like a fool, then asked, "When?"

"I'm ready tomorrow," Jessica declared.

Yancy thought on that and nodded.

"No use waiting," he mused. "Tomorrow works for me."

Surprise filled Jessica's face.

"I didn't actually mean tomorrow, Yancy. It was just a figure of speech."

"Oh."

"However," Jessica looked thoughtful, "there isn't any reason to wait. Do you really *want* to get married tomorrow?"

"You bet I do."

Excitement glowed in Jessica's eyes as she looked at Tussle.

"Any objections?"

Tussle was still stunned, but he recovered and tried to make sense of it all.

"A few," he said gruffly. "For starters, where will you live?"

"We have a house in town," Yancy spoke up.

"More like a shack," Tussle corrected. "Besides, you, Cooper, and Josie already live there. *And* Wyatt when he's in town."

"Other arrangements will be made soon," Yancy replied, and he glanced at Jessica. "Are you fine with that?"

"Of course!" Jessica flashed him a grin.

Yancy returned the grin and looked back at Tussle.

"Anything else?"

Tussle wasn't done yet.

"Can you support her?"

"I'll do whatever it takes," Yancy declared.

"Oh, we'll be *just* fine," Jessica interrupted before Tussle could reply. "Things will work out. They always do."

Yancy and Jessica grinned at each other some more, and Tussle scowled and shook his head.

"Well, I tried," he mumbled.

"No more objections?" Jessica looked at him.

"Will it do any good?" He asked.

Jessica laughed and shook her head.

"Fine," Tussle grumbled. "You two deserve each other."

"Tomorrow it is then," Jessica declared.

Yancy stood, and he looked excited and awkward at the same time.

"Tomorrow evening?" He suggested.

Jessica nodded her acceptance.

"That should give you enough time to take a bath and shave," she advised.

"I already had a bath."

"Another one won't hurt," Jessica urged.

"I reckon I *could* use a shave," Yancy mused.

"I would appreciate that," Jessica said, and her eyes twinkled at him.

CHAPTER EIGHT

The tension in the room was gone. Yancy and Jessica ignored us as they finalized their wedding plans, and I'd never heard Yancy talk so much.

Jessica suddenly uttered a cry of alarm. Everyone in the room was startled, and we all looked at her.

"Your arm!" She pointed. "You're wounded!"

I heaved a sigh, crossed my arms, and leaned back in my chair.

"Yes," Yancy's face suddenly turned grave. "I am. But don't worry; it's just a scratch now."

"What happened?" Jessica's eyes were large and round.

"Just some hand to hand combat."

"Against who?"

"Apaches."

Jessica was obviously excited.

"*Apaches*! How many?"

"We went up against three."

"And you killed them all?"

"Sure did," Yancy beamed.

"With a little help from me," I added sourly, and I shot Yancy a dark look.

"Yes, you were there," Yancy admitted.

"I'm glad you remembered," I replied.

Yancy frowned at me and looked back at Jessica, who was shaking her head in wonder.

"I can only imagine what you went through," she said.

"Yes, *we* went through quite an ordeal," I said, and then I stood. "Think I'll go see what Wyatt's up to."

Nobody replied. A few seconds passed, and I grunted and started to leave the room. However, I stopped abruptly when I noticed my chair.

A brown outline of dirt was displayed on the white cushion, *exactly* where I'd been sitting. It was very noticeable, and my eyes grew wide.

I swept the chair with my hand several times. However, my attempts only made it look worse.

"I'm sorry about this," I said, embarrassed.

There was no reply.

I looked up. Yancy and Jessica were grinning at each other again, and Tussle was watching them with a frown.

"Sorry about this," I tried again, but nobody acknowledged me.

I looked back at the now *brown* chair. Then I shrugged, put my hat on, and walked out.

CHAPTER NINE

I stepped out onto the porch and looked down at the barn.

The cowpunchers had finished their nightly chores. They had also cleaned up and changed clothes, and they were playful and joking with each other as they saddled their horses.

Wyatt was saddling up too, and he and Tex were laughing about something. As I watched them, I couldn't help but feel a pinch of envy.

I walked down to the corrals. Wyatt spotted me, and he and Tex came over.

"Coop," Wyatt said. "This is Tex."

Tex really was big as a mountain, and I felt like a child standing next to him. He had broad, muscular shoulders, a boyish like face, and long, bowed legs. In fact, his legs were so bowed, if straightened, he would have been even taller.

Tex gave me a big, good-natured smile and extended his hand. We exchanged a firm handshake, and I tried not to grimace as he squeezed the blood out of my hand.

"Heard a lot about you, boss," he said in a friendly, Texas drawl. "You and your brother have quite the reputation."

He released my hand, and I felt a tingling sensation as blood flowed back into my fingers.

"We get around," I said, and I dropped my hand to my side and shook it slightly.

He nodded. His face was friendly and genuine, and I couldn't help but like him.

"Wyatt told me about you and Yancy rescuing him from the Apaches. That was really something."

"Just doing our job," I shrugged.

"If I ever get in a fix like that, I hope you and Yancy are around."

"Sure thing," I said.

"Well," Tex drawled, and he playfully hit Wyatt on the shoulder. "Everybody's waiting. Reckon we'd best be on our way."

"Have a good evening," I said.

"You bet, boss."

Fearful of another handshake, I slipped my hands in my pockets and looked at Wyatt.

"Don't forget to come by," I reminded.

"I'll be there," Wyatt replied.

I nodded, and Wyatt and Tex walked over to their horses and swung into the saddle. They joined the others, and everyone nudged their horse forward.

I watched them trot out, and then I walked back up to the main house.

Tussle had followed me out. He was smoking a cigar on the porch, and I joined him.

"You've hired some new hands," I said.

"A few," Tussle replied.

"Tex seems interesting."

Tussle took a puff on his cigar and nodded.

"Good hand," he said. "Especially with horses."

"I heard that," I said wryly, then asked, "Where's he from?"

"He didn't say; I didn't ask."

"Seems friendly."

"He is, mostly."

"*Mostly*?" My curiosity was kindled.

Tussle was silent a moment, but then explained.

"He likes to pick up a bottle sometimes."

"Oh?" I narrowed my eyes.

"It's only when he's in town. I won't allow it here."

"*Every* time he's in town, or just sometimes?"

"That's the only reason he goes," Tussle replied.

I frowned at that and asked, "How often does this happen?"

32

"Every week. He never misses."

"And he drinks a lot?"

"Enough to sink a boat," Tussle confirmed.

I grunted my disapproval.

"So he gets drunk."

"Pretty much."

"Does he cause trouble?"

"Sometimes."

"How much?" I pressed.

"There was a fight a few weeks back. He broke some chairs, a window, a feller's arm, and a table."

I moaned and shook my head.

"Sounds like a good influence for Wyatt," I said disapprovingly.

"Tex *is* good for Wyatt out here," Tussle defended. "He's taught him a lot, and Tex says Wyatt has a lot of potential with horses."

I snorted, and it was silent as I thought the situation over.

"Sounds like Tex has a problem," I finally said.

"I'd say so."

"What drives him to drink?" I mused.

"Been pondering that myself," Tussle replied. "There's happy drunks, and then there's depressed drunks."

"Which sort is Tex?"

"The depressed sort," Tussle declared. "He's trying to forget something."

"Forget what?"

"Don't know," Tussle shrugged. "Whatever it is, it must be something painful."

I nodded slowly but didn't reply.

CHAPTER TEN

Tussle smoked two cigars before the two lovebirds finally came out of the house.

My brother displayed a goofy looking expression, and so did Jessica. They just stood there on the porch, looking at each other and grinning like school kids.

Finally, I grunted loudly and interrupted their stare. We moved to our horses, untied them, and climbed into the saddle.

"I'll see you tomorrow," Jessica said from the porch.

"Yes," Yancy drawled. "You sure will."

They grinned at each other some more. Yancy made no move to leave, so I nodded goodbye to Tussle and nudged my horse forward. Jug-head fell in behind, and Yancy reluctantly turned his horse and joined me.

We trotted in silence. We went a mile or so, and I looked over at Yancy.

He was still grinning like a fool.

"Interesting proposal," I commented.

Yancy looked sideways at me.

"It worked, didn't it?"

"It did at that."

"Tomorrow will be an interesting day."

"Yes, it should."

"Everything happened so fast!" Yancy exclaimed.

"Sure did," I replied. "One word led to another."

"And now I'm getting married."

"Looks like."

Yancy grinned, and we were silent as we trotted another mile. Then a thought occurred to me, and I pinched my face in deliberation.

"Tussle was his usual, jolly self," I commented.

"Sure was," Yancy agreed. His face darkened, and he added, "That's the only bad thing about this."

"What's that?"

"We're going to be family now."

"*You* will, but not me," I replied.

Yancy frowned at me, and I smiled. We traveled a bit further, and I cleared my throat.

"How does grass run out in more ways than one?" I asked.

Yancy glanced at me.

"What?"

"That's what Tussle said," I reminded.

"I don't recall that."

"Well, you *were* a bit busy," I replied, then added, "I can't figure what he meant. Cows eat grass, but there's something else too. Grasshoppers, perhaps?"

"I don't see any hopping around."

"Point taken."

Yancy thought a moment, then suggested, "Mebbe a grassfire?"

"We would have seen the burn," I disagreed.

"True," Yancy replied.

It fell silent again. It was obvious that Yancy's thoughts were elsewhere, and he seemed disinterested in the grass conversation.

I couldn't blame him. However, *I* wasn't the one getting married, and I couldn't stop pondering about it.

"Sort of a riddle," I finally said.

Yancy must not have heard me, because he looked at me with a suddenly somber expression.

"Speaking of Tussle, he made some good points," he said.

"Did," I agreed.

"What do you think?"

"About?"

Yancy frowned at me and asked, "Are we making a mistake, getting married all quick like?"

I thought a moment.

Then I said, "In times like these, it's probably best not to do that."

"Do what?"

"Think."

Yancy chuckled and nodded.

"Thanks," he said.

"Anytime."

CHAPTER ELEVEN

It was almost dark by the time we reached Midway. However, there were lights lit up and down the main street, and town was crowded and full of excitement.

"Friday night," Yancy commented, and I nodded.

Midway was mainly a cow town. But it was also a fast-growing town, and there were several new shops scattered up and down the street.

There was also another new building being built, and that was our very own Texas Ranger station. We pulled up and looked it over, and we were pleased with the progress.

The walls and roof were up, and the wooden floors were finished. However, there was no siding yet, and we could see all the way through the building. The prison cells were in the back, and by the looks of it were finished and ready for business.

A pot-bellied wood stove had been installed in the front room. It was nickel-plated and had several burners on top for cooking.

"You got your wood stove," I observed.

"Sure did," Yancy grinned.

"That thing's so big, it looks like they had to build the office *around* it," I said.

"Come December, you'll be proud to have it," Yancy declared.

I nodded in agreement and looked the rest of the building over.

"Going to be bigger than I thought," I commented.

Yancy nodded and gestured at a side room that was beside the office.

"That'll be the living quarters," he said. "That's where Jessica and I will live."

I raised an eyebrow.

"Is that the 'other arrangements' you were talking about?"

"Yep, I've got it all figured out," Yancy replied smugly. "We'll live here, and you, Josie, and Wyatt can have the house."

I frowned at that.

"So, when we're freezing in December, you and Jessica can stay warm beside the new wood stove," I said disapprovingly.

"You're not as cold natured as I am," Yancy reminded.

"How thoughtful of you."

Yancy grinned and changed the subject.

"You gonna take a bath?"

I sniffed the air and pinched my face.

"Reckon I should?"

"Josie would appreciate it," Yancy replied, then offered, "Go on down to the bathhouse. I'll tend to your horse."

"You'd do that for me?" I raised an eyebrow.

"It ain't for you, it's for Josie."

I scowled, and Yancy grinned again as we dismounted.

CHAPTER TWELVE

Half an hour later, I was all cleaned up. My freshly shaved face itched as I joined Yancy, and we walked down the street.

Our house was on the edge of town. It was small but comfortable, and we could see a light burning inside the kitchen.

"Josie must be cooking supper," Yancy said, his voice flat with disappointment.

"What's wrong with that?" I challenged.

"You know."

"Reckon I do," I admitted, and I gestured at the front of our house. "Josie has company."

A saddled horse stood in the street, tied to the hitching rail. I didn't recognize the horse, and my curiosity was kindled as I wondered who it was.

We stepped up onto the porch, and we could smell a pleasant aroma coming from inside.

"I can't understand it," Yancy remarked.

"What?" I looked at him.

"Something smells *good*," he said, and I scowled at him. Yancy grinned and added, "Should we knock?"

"What for?" I replied. "It's *our* house."

I opened the door abruptly and walked in. I heard a surprised gasp, and I spotted Josie in the kitchen. Another lady was with her, and they both had aprons on.

A pleased look crossed Josie's face when she recognized us.

I might be a bit biased, but in my opinion, my wife was the prettiest thing that had ever come along. She had a sharp, young-looking face with long, brown hair. And, underneath her appearance was an undeniable strength that I had always admired.

She had lived an interesting life. Apaches captured her when she was young, and she had lived with them until recently.

But that was in the past. She was *my* wife now, and we got along just fine.

"We're home!" I announced.

A happy smile crossed Josie's face. She hurried towards me, and I rushed to meet her.

CHAPTER THIRTEEN

Josie and I embraced. She felt mighty good in my arms, and I was flooded with emotion.

A few seconds passed, and I reluctantly let her go.

Josie grabbed my hand and led me to the kitchen. Yancy followed, and Josie introduced us to her company.

The lady's name was Emily Basset. She was young, probably in her early twenties, and she had a frail figure and brown hair. She was also shy, and she looked down at the floor when she talked.

"Emily and her husband moved here last year," Josie told us. "They live a few miles outside of town."

"On a ranch?" I asked pleasantly, keeping the conversation going.

"Yes, my husband bought the Hoye spread," Emily spoke up. "It's a small place that needs a lot of work."

"I've heard of it," I replied. "I believe it borders J.T. Tussle's land."

"It does," Emily confirmed. She hesitated, then added, "My husband and Mr. Tussle know each other."

Her face turned wistful as she said it, and it kindled my curiosity.

"Oh?" I prompted.

An embarrassed look crossed her face.

"We've had trouble," she said.

"What sort of trouble?"

Emily looked down at the floor and didn't reply. A few awkward seconds passed, and I glanced at Yancy and looked back at her.

"Perhaps we could help," I said gently. "After all, we *are* Texas Rangers."

Emily looked up. She studied me a moment, and then decided to explain.

"We can't keep our cattle on our own range," she said. "Mr. Tussle has more grass, so our cattle drift over there. As soon as we drive them home, they just go back."

So that's the answer to my riddle, I thought.

I looked at Yancy.

"There goes my grasshopper theory," I said, and Yancy nodded.

"I'm sorry?" Emily looked confused.

"Your husband does have a problem," I replied as I turned my attention back to her. "What's he doing about it?"

"Not a lot, I'm afraid. My husband claims it's free range, but Mr. Tussle disagrees. They've had arguments."

I frowned at that.

"Your husband is misinformed, ma'am," I said.

"If it would just rain," Emily said, her face strained.

"That would help," I agreed.

Emily started to reply, but another thought occurred to her. Her eyes grew wide, and a hand flew to her face.

"Is it dark outside?" She asked.

"Yes, ma'am, just about."

"Oh no! I'm so late!"

"Do you need help?" I offered.

"No, I just have to go," she said, and she removed her apron and hurried toward the door. "My husband will be furious!"

"Nice meeting you," I called after her, but she didn't hear me.

Yancy joined me at the door, and we watched as she untied her horse, jumped on, and left town in a brisk trot.

"Interesting lady," I commented.

Yancy nodded and added, "Her husband doesn't know much about ranching."

"Sounded like," I agreed.

"It's a wonder Tussle hasn't shot him," Yancy remarked as I shut the door. "Dry as it is, Tussle needs all the grass he has."

"Perhaps we should talk to Emily's husband," I suggested.

Yancy nodded his agreement.

"Might save his life," he said.

I returned the nod and looked at Josie.

"Do you know the Bassets well?"

"Only Emily. She is my friend," Josie declared.

I was glad to hear that. The town folks still hadn't warmed up to Josie, and she was always alone when I wasn't around.

"Everyone could use a friend," I smiled warmly at her.

"Emily's husband is a bad man," Josie declared, and her eyes flashed in anger. "Indian braves treat their squaws better."

"He mistreats Emily?" Yancy asked.

Josie nodded.

"Yes."

Yancy frowned. He scratched his jaw and glanced at me.

"Emily's a pretty little thing," he commented.

"Sure is," I agreed. Josie frowned at me, and I quickly added, "But not near as pretty as *you*."

Josie ignored my comment.

"Will you help her?"

"Can't, unless she asks for it," I replied, then asked, "Just how bad is it?"

"Bad."

"Yes, but *how* bad?"

"Bad enough."

I sighed. Between Josie and Yancy, our conversations were usually abrupt and one worded.

"I'm afraid '*bad enough*' isn't '*good enough,*'" I replied, and I smiled at my play on words.

Josie missed my humor.

"She won't say anything," she said. "But, I've seen bruises."

"We'll nose around, and see if there's anything we can do," Yancy spoke up.

"Good," Josie declared, and she gestured at the kitchen and announced proudly, "Emily is teaching me to cook!"

"You don't say?" I raised an eyebrow.

There was a pot of stew on the stove. I walked over, picked up the ladle, and sampled it.

"Say!" My face lit up. "This is pretty good. Did you make this?"

"No, Emily did."

"Oh," my face fell.

CHAPTER FOURTEEN

Yancy made a pot of coffee, and we tore into the stew with a vengeance.

While we ate, I told Josie where we'd been and what all had happened. I finished by explaining about our visit to Tussle's headquarters.

Josie gasped and looked at Yancy.

"*You* are getting married?"

Yancy started to reply, but I beat him to it.

"Shocking, I know," I said. "Apparently, miracles *do* happen."

Yancy pursed his lips, and I smiled at him.

It was a lot to take in, and Josie shook her head in wonder as I ate my last bite. I sighed in contentment and pushed my chair back

"This was wonderful," I said, then added, "I'll help with the dishes. Wyatt should be here soon."

"Wyatt's in town?" Josie was startled.

"He rode in with Tussle's crew."

"Where is he then?"

"He's around somewhere," I replied. "I told him to come home early. He needs to talk to you."

"About?"

I hesitated, wondering how to answer that, and I finally decided to avoid it.

"I'll let Wyatt explain," I said.

Josie frowned at that, but didn't reply.

We cleaned up, and Yancy made another pot of coffee. We sat around the table and visited, and we drank the whole pot.

An hour passed, and I began to wonder where Wyatt was. I voiced my displeasure, and Yancy offered to go look for him.

I shook my head stubbornly.

45

"Nope," I declared. "I'm going to sit right here and wait for him."

"Mind if I turn in?" Yancy asked.

"Go ahead," I said. "No sense all of us losing sleep."

Yancy nodded, and he went to the bedroom while Josie and I went to the front room. We sat beside each other and settled in to wait.

Now that we were alone, we suddenly had a lot to discuss. We talked on and on, and I lost all sense of time.

Several hours passed, and it was past midnight when I heard a noise at the door.

It was Wyatt.

He slipped in and shut the door. He held his hat in his hand and had his head ducked low.

"Well," I declared. "It's about time you showed up. Where've you been?"

"I was with the boys."

"Doing what?" I challenged.

"Tex was teaching me how to play poker," Wyatt said, excitement in his voice. "We got a game going, and I won five dollars!"

I frowned my displeasure.

"So you're a gambler now too?"

"I lost track of time," Wyatt murmured.

I stared at him, and several seconds ticked by.

If it hadn't been so late, I would have told him a thing or two. However, I suddenly noticed how exhausted I was, I needed sleep and time to think.

"Well, you two can talk if you want," I said as I stood. "I'm going to bed."

"I'm sorry," Wyatt said earnestly.

"We'll discuss this tomorrow," I said, then added, "But, your behavior is disappointing. Especially after the talk we had today."

Wyatt looked remorseful. He acted like he wanted to say something, but I ignored him as I headed toward the bedroom.

"Good night," I said over my shoulder.

Part Two
"Yancy and Jessica's Wedding Day"

CHAPTER FIFTEEN

It seemed I had hardly crawled into bed and closed my eyes when a loud, irritating, and constant thumping sound woke me.

I grunted, forced my eyes open, blinked, and looked around.

It was dark. Josie was asleep beside me, and Yancy and Wyatt were across the bedroom in their beds.

Someone was knocking on our front door.

Yancy sat up. We looked at each other, and we crawled out of our beds, grabbed our Colts, and headed toward the front room.

"Who is it?" I asked, irritation in my voice.

"It's me, Sheriff Wagons!" replied a frantic voice.

I scowled and opened the door.

"Don't you know what time it is?" I asked roughly.

"It's three in the morning," Wagons replied, missing the point.

He was disturbed and upset. I gestured for him to come inside, and I shut the door behind him.

All the commotion woke up Josie and Wyatt. Josie lit a lantern, and they shuffled into the room while Sheriff Wagons just stood there, looking like he might cry.

Jason Wagons was the sheriff of Midway. He was around twenty years old, and he was chubby with fair skin and red cheeks.

Sheriff Wagons was known as the man who killed Stew Baine, and it was this reputation that helped him defeat Yancy in the sheriff's election several months back. They weren't very fond of each other, so I knew something had to be bad wrong for him to be here.

"What is it, Wagons," I asked flatly, silently wishing I could go deaf before he replied.

His voice quivered.

49

"There's a drunk in the saloon."

"Happens often in saloons," I answered.

"But this one is *really* mean."

"Why don't you arrest him then," I suggested.

"I tried," he whimpered. "But he took my gun away. I tried to get it back, and he picked me up and threw me across the room."

I suddenly noticed that his lower lip was bloody, and there was a nasty looking welt forming on the side of his face.

"Who is this feller?" I asked, fearful I already knew the answer.

"He rides for Mr. Tussle. Real big fella. He's caused problems before."

I felt a sinking feeling. I glanced at Wyatt, and his eyes were wide.

"Tex?" I asked.

"Yeah, that's him," Wagons nodded.

I made a small groaning sound.

"What are we going to do?" Wagons looked anxious.

"You're the sheriff, not us," I pointed out. "It ain't our problem."

"You won't help me?" A terrified look crossed his face.

I sighed and looked at Yancy.

"What do you say?"

Yancy frowned in thought.

"Wouldn't look good, us sleeping while he's tearing up the town," he said.

I nodded reluctantly, and Yancy turned to Wagons.

"Go keep an eye on him. We'll be there soon as we get dressed."

"I can't thank you enough," Wagons said, obviously relieved.

I opened the door and said, "No, you can't."

"And I'll help if you need it," Wagons added.

"That's comforting," I said.

Sheriff Wagons nodded emphatically and left. I shut the door, and I grumbled to myself as Yancy and I went to the bedroom and crawled into our clothes.

A thought occurred to me, and I walked over to the corner and picked up a new ax handle I had bought several months back. I handled it some and grunted my satisfaction.

Yancy was watching me.

"That's a good idea," he said. "Got one for me?"

"Sorry," I shook my head. "You're on your own."

Yancy frowned his disappointment, but he said no more as he turned and walked out.

Josie and Wyatt had followed us to the bedroom, and they were concerned. Wyatt looked like he wanted to say something, but he decided not to.

"We'll be back," I told Josie, then added, "I hope."

"Be careful," Josie replied.

I smiled reassuringly at her. Then I looked at my bed with something close to lust, and followed after Yancy.

CHAPTER SIXTEEN

"How did Wagons ever manage to kill Stew Baine?" Yancy asked as we walked down the street. "He can't even handle one drunk."

"I've wondered that myself," I replied as I yawned.

"Lee Mattingly knows something," Yancy declared. "He always just smiles when I mention it."

It was still a touchy subject for Yancy, but I had other things on my mind. I coughed and changed the subject.

"Whatever happens, we can't kill him," I said.

"Who? Wagons?"

"No," I corrected. "Tex."

"We're entitled to defend ourselves," Yancy objected.

"Wyatt looks up to Tex," I explained. "We kill him, and Wyatt will never talk to me again."

"Oh," Yancy said, then shrugged. "Surely it won't come to that. We've handled drunks before."

"Not as big as Tex."

"Bigger they are, the harder they fall."

"I'll remember you said that."

"We just have to move in quick like and grab him," Yancy instructed. "We'll take him down before he knows what happened."

"I'll follow your lead," I said as we stepped up onto the porch. "After all, *you're* the expert when it comes to hand to hand combat."

Yancy frowned at me, and we pushed through the batwing doors. We stopped just past the doorway while our eyes adjusted, and then we looked around.

It was a fancy place. There was a long, mahogany bar on one side, and there were several tables strung out in the middle. There were some pool tables in the back, and behind that was the poker room.

This saloon had a lot of history. Most notably, it was where Ben Kinrich had killed our good friend, Chino.

As expected, the saloon was empty.

Tex stood at the bar, and he was drinking whiskey straight from a bottle. His face was dark and ugly, and his eyes had a wild, crazed look.

He turned and glared at us. There was no recognition in his face; he was probably too drunk to remember us.

There were several shattered chairs scattered about, and the floor was covered with broken glass. I also spotted a gun handle sticking out of a spittoon, and I figured it was Sheriff Wagons' Colt.

As for our honorable Sheriff, he was hiding in the corner, and the bartender stood by the piano.

The bartender's name was Bart. He was a big, muscular man who had handled his share of drunks. However, this time he was covering his bloody nose with a handkerchief, and his right eye was swelling.

"You all right?" Yancy asked him.

"No," Bart replied sourly. "You might have to shoot him."

"We'll see," Yancy said, and we turned our attention to Tex.

He displayed a savage, wicked grin. He seemed eager to fight, and he silently invited us to try something.

"He ain't armed," I said softly.

"Too bad," Yancy replied, then asked, "You ready?"

"Not really," I admitted.

"Let's go then."

I nodded, and we walked toward the bar.

CHAPTER SEVENTEEN

We were careful not to make any threatening movements. We approached Tex, and he never even flinched. Instead, he watched us silently as we spread out in front of him.

Several seconds passed, and the silence was loud. Finally, Yancy cleared his throat.

"You need to come with us," he said.

Tex didn't move or say anything. He just continued to stare at us.

"I don't think he heard you," Wagons said from his corner.

Yancy frowned. He glanced at me and looked back at Tex.

"Let's go," he said, and he reached out, grabbed Tex's arm, and gave a little tug.

With catlike reflexes, Tex yelled, swung his fist, and connected a staggering blow to Yancy's face.

Yancy stumbled backwards, and Tex leaped forward. He grabbed Yancy by the shirt, picked him up with ease, and flung him across the room.

Yancy yelled as he took flight, and he landed in the middle of a table. It shattered, and wood splinters flew everywhere.

Tex's face was in a rage. He started to turn towards me, but I jumped forward and swung my ax handle.

I hit him hard between the shoulders, and he gasped and took a small step. Before he could recover, I hit him again across the ear, and the ax handle shattered in my hands.

Tex managed to stay on his feet. He staggered a few steps, shook his head several times, and uttered a groan. Then he collapsed and landed on top of Yancy, who was struggling to get up.

It was a nasty fall, and I grimaced as Yancy disappeared underneath Tex.

Tex was out cold. His body was limp, and I hurried over and peered down.

"Yancy!" I called out. "You alive under there?"

"Just get him off!" Came the muffled reply.

I grabbed Tex's leg and tugged.

"You were right," I gasped. "The bigger they are, the harder they *do* fall."

Yancy chose not to reply as I grunted and pulled.

CHAPTER EIGHTEEN

Sheriff Wagons and Bart hurried over, and it took all three of us to drag Tex off.

"You all right?" I asked as Yancy struggled to sit up.

Yancy looked dazed. He touched his face gingerly and winced.

Already, I could see a nasty bruise forming, and his eye was bright red.

"Hurts," Yancy muttered.

"I can't imagine why," I replied, and I reached down, grabbed Yancy's arm, and helped him up.

He swayed a bit, but stayed on his feet.

"If'n I was you, I'd take that bandage off your arm and wrap it around your face," I suggested.

Yancy was mad. He glared at me, and I could tell he was about to go to his grunt and one word replies.

"Let's get Tex to his cell before he wakes up," I suggested.

The four of us grabbed a leg or arm and picked him up. Yancy wasn't much help, but he tried.

Tex was heavy. We stumbled out the door and went down the street, and progress was slow.

The new Texas Ranger station was closer than the jail, and I gestured at it with my head.

"Let's take him there," I gasped.

I received no objections, and we struggled across the street. There was no door yet, so we went through the opening and made our way to the back. We dropped Tex in the closest cell, and Yancy slammed the door shut.

"I hope they've made keys," I commented.

Yancy grunted and turned away. Meanwhile, I studied Tex to make sure he was breathing, and I was relieved when I saw his chest going up and down.

"He's alive," I announced. "He just needs to sleep it off."

"He'll have plenty of time for that," Yancy muttered.

"Need me for anything else?" Bart spoke up.

"Nope," I said. "'Preciate the help."

"Anytime," Bart replied, then left.

I turned to Wagons.

"You can go too," I told him.

Wagons nodded and looked at Yancy.

"Sorry about your face," he said.

Yancy didn't reply, and several awkward seconds passed. Wagons glanced at me, and I gestured for him to leave. He nodded, looked back at Yancy once more, and then left.

I turned to Yancy. He was just standing there, looking sullen.

"Well, nothing else we can do right now," I said. "We might as well go back to bed."

Yancy didn't reply. But he did nod, and we walked out the door and headed toward our house.

"We'll write out a report in the morning," Yancy said suddenly.

"Report?" I raised an eyebrow.

Yancy nodded.

"We'll need one for the trial."

"Trial?" I made a face. "What for?"

"Attempted murder."

"Aw, it wasn't *that* bad."

"We'll add destroying private property, disturbing the peace, assault, and anything else we can think of."

"Let's not make hasty decisions," I urged.

Yancy grunted, and the conversation came to an abrupt end.

Josie and Wyatt were waiting for us. Their mouths fell open when they saw Yancy, but he ignored them as he walked to the bedroom.

"What happened?" Josie turned to me.

I explained, and Wyatt looked anxious.

"What's going to happen to Tex?" He asked.

"Don't know yet."

"I'm sure he didn't mean it. He just had too much to drink."

I smiled at that.

"He meant it, all right," I replied. Then, before Wyatt could reply, I added, "We'll figure it out in the daylight. Right now, my bed is calling me."

Wyatt frowned his displeasure, but I was in no mood to argue. I went to the bedroom, undressed, and crawled into bed. I was out as soon as my head hit the pillow, and I slept hard.

CHAPTER NINETEEN

It was still dark when I woke up. I sat up, yawned, and looked around the bedroom.

Yancy was still snoring, but Josie and Wyatt were awake. I made a motion for them to keep quiet, and we crawled into our clothes and eased out of the room.

"Let him sleep," I told them. "He probably needs it."

They nodded their agreement. We went to the kitchen, and Josie built a fire in the stove. As soon as there were coals, I made some coffee and cooked scrambled eggs and biscuits.

I placed the food on the table, and we sat in our usual chairs.

Wyatt looked sullen, Josie was her usual quiet self, and I was irritable over lack of sleep. There wasn't any conversation while we ate, and the silence was uncomfortable.

After breakfast, I made a plate for Tex and poured him a cup of coffee. Before I left, I looked at Wyatt.

"Have a good talk last night?" I asked.

"With who?" Wyatt replied.

I scowled. I nodded towards Josie, and Wyatt shook his head.

"Not so much," he admitted.

"Well, now is as good a time as any," I declared.

Josie looked confused, but I figured Wyatt could explain it better than I could. I gave Wyatt a stern look, and he nodded somberly.

I gave Josie a comforting smile. Then, I picked up Tex's breakfast, stepped outside, and walked down the street.

It was a cool morning, and the breeze was pleasant. It was also a Saturday, so no one would be working on the Texas Ranger station.

I walked through the open doorway and saw Tex sitting on his bunk.

I stopped and studied him a moment.

He was holding his head, and he looked depressed. In fact, it looked like he had been crying. His eyes were puffy, and his ear was swollen.

I cleared my throat to get his attention, and he looked up as I walked over.

"Cooper," he said softly.

"Glad you recognize me," I replied, and I handed him his breakfast through the opening of the cell.

He took a swig of coffee and winced as he swallowed.

"What happened last night, boss?"

"You don't remember?" I stared at him.

He shook his head, embarrassed.

"'Fraid not," he said, then added, "It feels like somebody worked me over good."

"Only twice."

"What happened?"

"You sure you want to know?"

"Probably not," he said, his voice soft. "But go ahead."

I told him everything, and recollection flashed in his eyes.

"I remember now," he said. He frowned and added, "You don't fight right."

"You're the one who was on the ground," I reminded.

A faint smile crossed his lips.

"I was at that," he admitted.

Tex sighed. He shook his head slowly, and there was true regret in his eyes.

"I'm so sorry," he muttered. "Is Yancy all right?"

"He's still asleep."

"I'd like to see him."

"Don't worry; you will soon enough."

"Is he upset?"

"Just a touch."

60

"He has a right to be," Tex muttered. "I'm such a fool."

"I won't argue with that," I agreed. A few seconds passed, and I changed the subject. "While we have a moment, there's something else I'd like to discuss."

"Yes, boss?"

"It's about Wyatt."

Tex's face lit up.

"He's a good boy," he said.

"I don't want you around him," I announced abruptly.

Tex's face fell. His lower lip quivered, and he looked like he might cry again.

"Please don't say that," he said.

"You ain't what I'd call a good influence," I replied. "Just look at yourself."

"I know," he said. "But you don't understand."

"Enlighten me then."

Tex paused while he searched for the right words.

"Wyatt is all I've got," he admitted. "He keeps me going, and he gives me something to live for."

"I'm sorry, but that's not good enough."

"But I'm a different person when I'm around him," Tex insisted.

I sighed and pinched my face in thought. It was silent a moment, and Tex looked desperate while he waited for me to say something.

"We'll talk more later," I finally said.

Tex looked grateful, and he nodded his thanks.

I returned the nod, and I watched as he tore into his breakfast.

"Why do you do it?" I asked suddenly.

"Do what, boss?" Tex looked up at me.

"Drink."

A pained expression crossed his face. It fell silent, and for a moment I thought he might not answer.

But then he said softly, "To forget."

"Forget what?" I pressed.

He hesitated, and then shrugged.

"Can't remember," he lied.

I frowned at that.

"It must be working then," I said, and I turned and left.

CHAPTER TWENTY

I went back to the house, and I could feel tension in the kitchen as soon as I walked in.

Josie stood by the stove; her face tight and drawn. Wyatt stood in the doorway, and he was looking at the floor.

I studied them a moment, and then I spotted Yancy. He was sitting at the table, drinking coffee and attempting to eat breakfast.

His appearance was startling, and I gasped.

His right eye was completely swollen shut. The entire side of his face was puffy, and his nose was red and inflamed.

"My, my," I said. "You all right?"

Yancy was in a sour mood.

He grunted and said, "Just let me drink my coffee, and no one will get hurt."

"Is your nose broken?" I stared at it.

"Don't know. Hurts too much to touch."

"Want me to twist on it some?" I offered.

"I do not."

I nodded. Yancy took a swig of coffee, and he winced as he swallowed.

"Hurts?" I asked.

He nodded and said, "That table was hard."

"You *did* fly through the air," I grinned, then added, "I came off a horse like that once."

Yancy grunted in response.

"Still getting married today?" I asked.

Yancy scowled, or at least I thought it was a scowl, and looked at me.

"'Course I am. Why shouldn't I?"

"You sure you feel up to it?" I asked.

"I'll be fine."

"What about your face?"

"What about it?"

I scratched my jaw and frowned.

"Have you looked in a mirror this morning?"

"No. Why? Should I?"

I glanced at Josie and looked back at Yancy.

"I wouldn't," I said.

Yancy grunted and took another swig of coffee. Meanwhile, I took advantage of the silence and changed the subject.

"By the way; Tex said he was sorry."

Yancy narrowed his one good eye.

"He'll be sorry, all right," he declared.

"You haven't changed your mind?"

"Not hardly."

"What do you mean?" Wyatt spoke up.

I didn't reply, and Wyatt narrowed his eyes.

"Will Tex go to prison?"

"It's possible," I said.

"You can't do this," Wyatt objected.

"No, but Judge Parker can," Yancy smiled wolfishly at the thought.

"You just don't know Tex," Wyatt tried again. "He's a good fella when he's not drinking."

"Oh, I know him," Yancy muttered. "I got to know him up close and personal last night."

Wyatt glared at us, and a look of contempt crossed his face. He started to say something, but stopped. He turned abruptly, stormed out, and slammed the door behind him.

"What's wrong with *him*?" Yancy grunted and looked at me.

I didn't reply. I looked at Josie, and several seconds passed.

"This parenting thing is harder than I thought," I finally said.

"Should you go after him?" Josie asked.

"Best let him calm down first," I replied.

"He doesn't want us to be his parents," Josie announced.

Her face was emotionless. However, I could tell she was hurting on the inside, and I felt sorry for her.

"Did Wyatt say that?" I asked.

"Yes."

I snorted and shook my head.

So much for breaking it to her gently, I thought.

CHAPTER TWENTY-ONE

Whenever Yancy and I were in town, our morning routine was to make another pot of coffee after breakfast, sit out on the porch, and watch the town wake up.

This morning was no different.

Yancy placed a fresh pot of coffee on a small table between us. He sat, poured us both a cup, added three spoonfuls of sugar to his, and stirred. Then we picked up our cups, took deep swigs, and sighed in contentment.

If anything could revive Yancy's spirits, it was coffee. He leaned back in his chair, tilted his head, and allowed himself to relax.

"Coffee can't cure everything, but it sure helps," he remarked.

"Nobody makes it like you," I replied.

"Josie can't?"

"No," I said truthfully. "She can't."

"Have you tried teaching her?"

"A few times, actually."

"And?" Yancy prompted.

"It's worse now than it was."

"Perhaps Emily can help."

"One can only hope."

The thought of burned coffee was almost more than Yancy could tolerate. He shook his head slowly and looked sympathetic.

"I'm sorry," he said, and added, "But, *you* married her."

"What was I thinking," I said wryly. A thought occurred to me, and I asked, "Can Jessica make coffee?"

A worried look crossed Yancy's face.

"You know, I'm not exactly sure."

"Too late now," I said.

Yancy didn't reply, and I chuckled and took another swig.

After that we just sat there, and neither one of us spoke. There was nothing uncomfortable with the silence; that's just how it was with Yancy and me.

I liked to smoke a pipe, especially in the mornings. I reached into my vest pocket, pulled my tobacco pouch out, and carefully packed my pipe. Next, I struck a match and lit it, and I took a deep puff as I returned my tobacco pouch to my pocket.

"Hard to believe," I said as I exhaled.

Yancy looked at me.

"What is?"

"My little brother, getting married today."

"Haven't we already discussed this?"

"I reckon we have."

"Well then. No need to plow that field again."

I smiled.

"I was *attempting* to say I'm real happy for you, Yancy," I said. "And for Jessica."

"Oh. Well thank you, Coop."

"But are you sure you can handle married life?" I continued.

Yancy shot me a dark look.

"If I recall correctly, you said I shouldn't think about it," he reminded.

"That was yesterday."

Yancy sighed. He considered it a moment, then said, "You seem to be doing just fine."

"But Josie ain't like most women," I pointed out.

"Neither is Jessica."

"True, but Jessica is a sensitive lady," I warned. "She has feelings, and she lets them be known. Now take Josie; she doesn't express her feelings so much."

"She seemed mighty upset when we disliked her cooking," Yancy disagreed.

"Cooking aside, she's a pretty tough gal. Just look at how she's handling everything with Wyatt."

Yancy thought on that, and then asked, "So what's your point?"

I took a puff on my pipe and frowned.

"Well, I'm not exactly sure now," I admitted.

Yancy started to reply, but stopped. He was looking down the street, and a curious look crossed his face.

I turned and looked.

Four Mexican men were riding into town. They were travel worn, covered in dust, and in need of a bath and shave. They all displayed Colts on their hips, and they had a hard look about them.

They were riding our way, but they stopped before reaching us. They dismounted, tied their horses to hitching rails, and went inside a saloon that also served up breakfast.

They moved with an arrogant swagger. It was a look we had seen before, and it usually meant trouble.

Yancy glanced at me.

"Ever see them before?" He asked.

"Not that I recall," I shook my head.

"I don't like it."

"Can't say I do either," I said.

"I wonder who they are."

I started to reply, but stopped myself. I looked at Yancy and frowned.

"Hold it right there," I said sternly.

"What?" Yancy looked at me.

"It's *your* wedding day," I reminded.

"So?"

"You've got better things to do than fret over strangers."

"But it's my responsibility," Yancy argued.

"Actually, it's not," I corrected. "Wagons is the sheriff. *We're* Texas Rangers."

Yancy snorted.

"Is that supposed to bring me comfort?"

"Just this once; let it go," I urged. "They're probably just passing through anyway."

68

"What if they aren't?"

I thought on that and sighed.

"If it makes you feel better, I'll nose around, ask a few questions," I offered.

Yancy nodded thoughtfully.

"Yes, go ahead and do that."

"Just as soon as I finish my pipe and coffee," I suggested.

"Of course," Yancy agreed, and we took another swig of coffee and sighed in contentment.

CHAPTER TWENTY-TWO

Midway started waking up. The streets grew crowded, and we nodded at folks as they hurried past us on their way to work.

We continued to sit on the porch. I finished my smoke, and Yancy made another pot of coffee.

I had just refilled my cup when I spotted a one-horse drawn buggy approaching. It was a light, simple made buggy, with only two wheels and one seat.

I squinted at it and recognized Emily Basset. She was sitting beside her husband, and there was a boy squeezed in between them.

Yancy saw them too, and we studied the family as they drew closer.

Emily's husband was a hard looking man. His face was twisted and mean, and there wasn't any kindness in him. He was tall and lanky, and he had quick, shifty eyes.

He didn't appear to be armed. I found that odd, because just about everybody carried a gun around Midway, which was mostly a good thing.

I looked at the boy next, and I figured he was around ten or eleven. Unfortunately for him, he favored his father. However, he displayed an eager grin as he took in the sights of town.

I looked at Emily last, and my eyes grew wide.

She had her face down, and a shawl was wrapped around her shoulders. However, even from where we were sitting, I could see a nasty bruise forming underneath her eye.

Yancy sat up and grunted softly. They passed by, but nobody looked at us.

"Did you see that?" I asked.

"Sure did," Yancy replied. "And I only have one good eye."

"Emily didn't mention having a son."

"I reckon she was in too big a hurry to leave," Yancy replied.

I nodded and said, "That bruise wasn't there last night either."

A thoughtful look crossed Yancy's face.

"You don't suppose she slipped?"

I frowned, looked at Yancy, and asked, "Did *you* slip?"

"Not hardly."

"Then I doubt she did either."

"You figure he hit her for being late?"

"What it looks like."

"Does, don't it."

We thought on that, and then I said, "I suppose we should find out."

"We should," Yancy agreed, then added, "While we're at it, we can also educate Emily's husband about range manners."

"Somebody needs to," I said.

"Well, you go ahead and do that," Yancy said as he took another swig of coffee and leaned back.

"Me?" I objected.

"Sure."

"What about *you*?"

"You just said it was my wedding day," Yancy reminded. "Besides, I've got things that need attending to."

"Such as?" I challenged.

"Got to talk to the pastor," Yancy replied. "If he can't marry us on short notice, then I'll ask Judge Parker. I also need some new clothes, *and* another bath and shave."

I pursed my lips as I studied Yancy's bruises.

"Shaving won't be easy with *that* face," I commented. "I'd let someone else attempt it."

"I plan to," Yancy replied, then asked, "So, will you handle it? You're a better talker than I am anyway."

"You were doing just fine yesterday," I pointed out.

Yancy frowned. He looked at me and waited.

"Fine," I grumbled. "I'll look into it."

"Thanks, Coop."

"Before, or after I talk to those other fellers?" I asked.

"Makes no difference to me. Just don't wait too long. They might leave town."

"Who? The Mexicans or the Bassets?"

"Both."

"I'll fit it all in somehow."

"'Preciate it," Yancy said.

CHAPTER TWENTY-THREE

We continued to sit there and contemplate things.

"When's Jessica coming to town?" I asked.

"Not until this afternoon," Yancy replied. "Tussle is bringing her."

"Why wait so long? She busy with something?" I asked curiously.

"Yes. She's sewing."

"Sewing what?"

"Her mother's wedding dress," Yancy explained. "She's determined to wear it, but it needs changes of some sort."

"Like adjustments?"

"Yeah, that's it. That's what she called it too."

"You don't know much about dresses," I observed.

"Never had much reason to," Yancy shrugged.

"Fair enough," I replied. I thought it over, and then added, "Jessica will need a place to change when she gets here."

"Probably will."

"She can use the house," I offered. "Josie would like that. It'd make her feel a part of things, and perhaps take her mind off Wyatt."

"That'll work," Yancy agreed, and then he changed the subject. "Speaking of Wyatt, what happened to his voice? It's all deep and low now."

"You noticed too?"

"*Sure* did," Yancy drawled. He grinned and added, "Wyatt *sure* does say 'sure' a lot too."

"*Sure* does," I grunted in agreement.

"Wyatt *sure* seemed upset when he left the house."

"That's 'cause he was."

"Figured out what you're going to say to him?"

"No."

"My parenting skills are limited," Yancy admitted. "But, I'm pretty sure the truth is the best way to go."

"Truth about what?" I looked at Yancy.

He frowned in thought.

"Well, anything you tell him, I reckon."

"Thanks for the words of wisdom," I grunted, then added, "Problem is, Wyatt doesn't want to hear *anything* I say. We're not his parents, and he's made that clear."

"But he still needs looking after."

"Don't tell him that," I grumbled.

Yancy smiled sympathetically, and we poured ourselves another cup of coffee. Yancy poured in his usual three spoonfuls of sugar and stirred, and we both took deep swigs.

I had just lowered my cup when I spotted Bart, the bartender, walking towards us. As he got closer, I saw that his right eye was swollen shut, just like Yancy's.

He looked irritable as he stopped in front of us.

"Bart," I said pleasantly.

Bart nodded. He studied Yancy's face, decided not to mention it, and looked at me.

"How's Tex?" He asked.

"Has a sore head," I replied.

Bart grunted and asked, "What's going to happen to him?"

"Still pondering that," I said.

"Same sort of thing happened a few weeks ago," Bart told us. "Tex gets real ugly when he's drunk."

"Really? We hadn't noticed."

Bart ignored my sarcasm.

"I can't afford for this to keep happening," he complained.

"I can see how you might feel that way," I nodded.

"So you'll do something?"

"We'll figure something out," I replied.

Bart studied us a moment.

74

Then he said, "I hope you do."

"We appreciate your confidence," I said.

"That's not the only reason I'm here," Bart changed the subject.

"Oh?" I raised an eyebrow.

Bart turned to Yancy.

"I was asked to deliver a message."

"From who?" Yancy asked.

"Four Mexicans that just rode in."

"We saw them," Yancy said.

"They asked if you were in town. I told them you were, and they said they're here to see you."

"About?"

"They didn't say," Bart replied. "But, I'd be careful. They seem eager for trouble."

Yancy glanced at me and looked back at Bart.

"Coop will be along," he said.

"But they want you."

"Coop can handle it."

Bart frowned at that, but he still nodded.

"What do you want me to tell them?" He asked.

"That you delivered the message."

"Anything else?"

"That'll do."

"All right, Yancy. Whatever you say."

"'Preciate it," Yancy said.

Bart nodded. He headed toward the saloon, and Yancy looked at me.

"What do you make of it?" He asked.

I scrunched my face in thought.

"Sounds like trouble," I replied. "And, as usual, it'll be up to *me* to get you out of it."

Yancy grunted in response, and we took another swig of coffee.

CHAPTER TWENTY-FOUR

It was midmorning when Yancy and I finally left the porch. Yancy went to find the pastor while I figured out which chore to tackle first.

I assessed the situation as I walked down the street.

The Mexican's horses were still tied to the hitching rail, and the Bassets had stopped at the blacksmith's shop. I didn't see the husband, but Emily and her son were standing beside the buggy.

I figured the Mexicans weren't going anywhere. I walked toward the blacksmith shop, which was also beside our new Texas Ranger station.

I didn't want Emily's husband to see us, so I circled into the alley and came up between the two buildings. Tex spotted me from his cell, and his face sharpened with curiosity.

"What are you up to, boss?" He asked as I passed underneath his window.

"Mind your own business," I replied curtly.

I felt Tex's curious eyes on me as I stopped at the corner of the blacksmith shop. Emily and her son were a few feet from me, and I cleared my throat to get their attention.

Emily was startled, and she spun around. She gasped, took a step back, tripped, and fell.

"I'm so sorry!" She exclaimed as she jumped to her feet.

"Don't be," I replied, then grinned. "I'm used to women falling over me."

She smiled and made a little half-laugh, and I suddenly realized just how pretty she really *was*.

"Can you come over here?" I gestured. "We need to talk."

A worried look crossed Emily's face. She glanced at the blacksmith shop and looked back at me.

"I'm waiting for my husband," she replied.

"It'll only take a minute," I pressed.

She stood there a moment, and then nodded as she came to a decision. She grabbed the boy's hand and hurried over, and we stepped into the alley.

"Who's this?" I smiled at the boy.

"This is Little Ben," Emily replied.

I extended my hand. Little Ben was surprised, and he shrunk back. But then he grinned sheepishly and shook my hand.

"Nice to meet you, son," I said, and he nodded.

"I'm sorry I left so abruptly last night," Emily spoke up.

"It was abrupt," I agreed with a smile.

"Josie and I have become good friends. I like her a lot."

"So do I," I said.

Emily smiled with me. But then her expression vanished as she looked down at the ground, and several awkward seconds passed.

"My brother and I noticed your black eye, ma'am," I broke the silence, my voice gentle.

"It's nothing," she said quickly. "I bruise easily."

"Most folks do," I replied.

I paused while I gathered my thoughts. I looked up, and I noticed that Tex was listening intently from the window.

I frowned at him and looked back at Emily.

"Did your husband hit you?"

"No," she said.

"Yes," Little Ben said at the same time.

A long, uncomfortable silence followed while they both looked at each other. I waited a moment and continued.

"Well, that covers most the possibilities," I said. "Now, which is it?"

Emily looked back down at the ground while Little Ben looked at me.

"Pa was drunk," he explained, then added, "Pa drinks a lot when he gets mad."

I nodded and asked, "This has happened before?"

"Yes," Little Ben said, then added bitterly, "I don't like him."

"*Little Ben*," Emily said, her voice sharp.

"Don't say things like that, son," I said.

Little Ben frowned his apology and nodded while Emily looked at me.

"Please," she pleaded. "Don't do this. You'll only cause trouble."

Before I could reply, there was a noise by the buggy, followed by a hard, curt yell.

"Emily! Where are you woman?"

Emily gasped. She gave me one, last desperate look, and she grabbed Little Ben's hand and hurried away.

"Here I am," she said as they stepped out into the street.

"I told you to stay with the buggy!"

"I'm so sorry."

"Get in, let's go. Now!"

I walked to the corner, and I watched from the shadows as Emily and Little Ben jumped into the buggy. Her husband untied the horse and climbed in beside her, and his movements were jerky and abrupt.

They moved down the street and stopped at the feed store. The husband jumped to the ground, spoke roughly to Emily, tied the horse to the hitching post, and disappeared inside.

I frowned thoughtfully as I turned in the alley and looked up at Tex.

His face was twisted in hate. He was gripping the bars of his cell, and his knuckles were white.

"What a coward," he muttered.

"Pretty much," I agreed.

"What will you do?"

"Don't know yet."

"But you'll do something?"

"We'll see," I replied.

Tex's face turned hard as stone, and he looked at me with a somber expression.

"If you don't," he said softly, "then I will."

I narrowed my eyes at that, but didn't reply.

We looked at each other some more. Then, Tex turned from the window and sat on his bunk. His face was dark and ugly.

I stood there a moment, and then I turned, walked out into the street, and headed toward the saloon.

CHAPTER TWENTY-FIVE

There were two saloons in Midway, and Bart owned them both. The one the Mexicans were in was at the end of town.

Oddly enough, the saloon was next to the church, and I had always found that amusing.

The church was the tallest building in town, mainly because of the tall steeple. It was painted white, and the brightness made the church stand out from the other buildings.

The church was at the very end of the street, facing the rest of the town, and I always thought it made a pleasant view when riding in from the west.

It was a long walk to the saloon. I carried my Henry rifle like I always did, and I also had my Colt revolver strapped around my hip.

I exchanged a few pleasantries as I passed some folks, and then I reached the feed store. Emily and Little Ben were sitting in the buggy, and I nodded at them.

"Ma'am," I said.

Emily looked concerned. She returned the nod, and I felt her eyes on me as I walked past them.

I reached the saloon and stepped up onto the porch. I studied the Mexican's horses, and then I pushed through the batwing doors.

Like I always did, I paused at the doorway and let my eyes adjust. Then, I took a slow look around.

This saloon wasn't as fancy. The bar was plain, and the room smelled of whiskey, sweat, and tobacco. It was also dark and musky feeling.

My gaze settled on the four Mexicans. They were sitting at the corner table in the back, and they had positioned themselves so they could see the entire room.

I walked to the bar. I held my rifle with the barrel pointed down, and my thumb rested on the hammer.

Bart was tending bar. I nodded at him, and he returned the nod as I passed by. I reached the end of the bar, stopped, and faced the Mexicans.

The Mexicans were watching my every move. I returned their look, and it was silent for several seconds.

They were a shabby dressed bunch. All four were chewing tobacco, and the only time they took their eyes off me was when they spat in the direction of the spittoon.

The closest one grunted his amusement when he noticed my Texas Ranger badge. He was dark, lean, and hard bodied, and he displayed a full set of white teeth as he sneered at me.

"You Yancy Landon?" He spoke gruffly in broken English.

I decided it was best if I kept the mood light.

"I consider that an insult," I jested with a wry smile. "Everybody knows I'm better looking than that."

A confused expression crossed his face. He didn't reply; instead, he just waited.

I sighed and answered more plainly, "No, I am not Yancy."

He frowned his disappointment.

"We are here to see Yancy Landon."

"You'll have to deal with me," I announced.

"Where is Yancy?" He tried again.

"Busy."

A defiant look crossed his face.

"We will not leave until we see Yancy Landon."

"What business do you have with him?" I pressed for information.

A wolfish grin split his lips, and his white teeth shone even more.

"We are here to kill him," he announced with pride.

I felt a sinking feeling.

Always somebody eager to ruin a good day, I thought.

CHAPTER TWENTY-SIX

The room went very silent. Everyone present stared wide-eyed at us while they waited for me to reply.

Several seconds passed, but it felt longer. I stared at the Mexicans, and they stared back.

"That so," I finally said, my voice flat.

"Yes, it is so," he declared.

"Sounds sorta personal," I noted.

"It is."

"Why?" I asked.

"*That* I will tell Yancy."

"No, you will tell me," I said firmly. "Now."

He narrowed his eyes at that. We stared at each other some more, but my determined look never wavered. Finally, his stubborn look softened.

"Yancy killed my cousin," he announced.

I frowned at that.

"Who was your cousin?"

"Rocca," he announced. He puffed out his chest and added, "I'm Carlos, his blood cousin."

"Rocca the Injun trader?" I asked.

"He traded with the Indians, yes."

I remembered Rocca, all right. He was a half-breed, and he had shot me in the shoulder in the New Mexico Mountains. Soon after that, Yancy killed him while trying to arrest him.

"It was a fair fight," I recalled.

"And I will kill Yancy in a fair fight," Carlos declared.

"Rocca was trading rifles to the Injuns," I argued. "He had to be stopped."

What Rocca was doing didn't seem to have any effect on Carlos, because he just shrugged in response.

I looked at the others.

"How 'bout these fellers?" I asked Carlos. "Is Rocca their cousin too?"

"No, they ride with me."

"And are they planning on killing Yancy?"

"Only if I don't."

"You know who I am?" I asked.

He shook his head.

"I'm Cooper Landon," I announced. "Yancy's brother."

Who I was did not impress Carlos. He just shrugged again, and I frowned my displeasure.

"You won't change your mind?" I asked.

"I will not," he declared.

I sighed softly.

"I'll tell Yancy," I said.

"We will wait until suppertime," Carlos said. "Then we will come looking."

"No need for that. I'll get back with you."

Carlos didn't reply. Instead, he leaned over the spittoon and spat out a long, brown stream of tobacco juice.

Silence filled the room. I glanced at Bart, and then I turned to leave.

Nobody said a word as I walked to the doorway and pushed through the batwing doors.

CHAPTER TWENTY-SEVEN

I spotted Yancy down the street. I gestured at him, and we met in front of the Texas Ranger station. We went inside, and Yancy looked excited.

"Just talked to the pastor," he said. "He agreed to marry us!"

"Congratulations," I said, then added, "He might have to do a funeral or two as well."

"Oh?"

I explained about Carlos, and then I told Yancy about my conversation with Emily.

As I talked, I noticed Tex from his cell. He was listening, and his interest perked when I mentioned Emily.

Yancy's expression turned somber, and he scratched his jaw as he thought things over.

"They rode here just to kill me?"

"You're a popular man," I nodded.

"I knew they were trouble."

"Your assessment was correct."

"But this is ridiculous," he muttered. "Why couldn't they be simple, normal outlaws? Then we could arrest them and be done with it."

"Sounded simple to me," I replied. "Carlos is looking for revenge."

"Well, I won't play along," Yancy declared abruptly.

"You won't?" I was surprised.

"It's not that I'm afraid of him."

"Didn't think you were," I replied.

"But this is *my* day, not his," Yancy said. "I won't allow him to ruin it."

"It's sorta his day too, Yancy," I reasoned. "He's been waiting a long time for a chance to kill you."

"Well, he'll just have to wait longer. And you're going to tell him that."

"Tell him what, exactly?" I asked, confused.

"To go home."

"He won't do that."

"'Course he will," Yancy replied. "You'll just have to reason with him."

"Reason?"

"Sure. You're the one who's good with words."

"I ain't *that* good."

"You can even tell him it's my wedding day."

"That won't make any difference to Carlos," I argued.

Yancy gave me an irritated look, but then a concerned expression crossed his face as another thought occurred to him.

"Sheriff Wagons," he said softly.

"What about him?" I asked.

"He finds out about this, he could mess things up and get himself killed."

"Not the man who killed Stew Baine," I scoffed.

"Go talk to him," Yancy ignored my sarcasm. "Send him out of town on an errand or something."

"An errand?" I made a face.

"Sure. Just think something up."

"How 'bout you handle it?" I suggested.

"I would, but I've got to buy some new clothes."

"Busy man," I frowned.

"Man only gets married once."

"That's the hope," I replied, and then I sighed. "Fine. I'll talk to Wagons."

"And Carlos?"

"Why not," I said flatly.

Yancy nodded his thanks, but then his face turned somber.

"We also need to do something about Emily," he said.

"We do," I agreed. "But what?"

"Be nice if we could shoot her husband."

I noticed Tex's eyes lit up when Yancy said that, and I frowned my disapproval.

"We can't do that," I objected.

"I know, but it's fun to think about."

Tex looked disappointed.

"I'll talk with her again," I offered. "*If* she agrees to press charges, we can arrest her husband before they leave town."

Yancy nodded slowly.

"Yes, why don't we do that."

"There's no *we* about it," I mumbled. "But, *I'll* do it."

"'Preciate it."

I grunted in response.

CHAPTER TWENTY-EIGHT

We started to leave, but Tex called out and got our attention.

We walked over to his cell. A cold expression crossed Yancy's face, and he crossed his arms as he stood there.

"What is it, Tex?" I asked.

"Would you mind if I built a fire in the wood stove?" He asked. "If somebody would bring me the makings, I'll even make us some coffee."

Yancy and I glanced at each other. We frowned in confusion and looked back at Tex.

"You're in a prison cell," I reminded.

Tex shrugged. He grabbed the cell door and pushed, and it swung open with ease.

"I reckon the locks haven't been installed yet," he replied.

Yancy and I were startled.

"How long have you known about this?" Yancy wanted to know.

"Since last night."

"And you didn't escape?"

"No."

"Why not?" Yancy demanded.

Tex shrugged.

"Where would I go?"

Yancy and I glanced at each other again while Tex shut the cell door and sat on his bunk. His face turned dark as he looked down at the floor.

"I keep thinking about Emily," he told us, then muttered, "How could a man hit a pretty little woman like that?"

"Not much of a man," I said.

"He doesn't deserve her," Tex declared.

I nodded my agreement.

Then, on a whim, I asked, "You ever been married, Tex?"

Tex was surprised by the question. Several seconds passed, and his face turned mulish.

"Was," he said.

"But not anymore?"

He shook his head.

"She died," he said softly.

"When did this happen?" I asked, surprised.

"Last year."

"I'm sorry," I said.

Tex nodded, and his face turned tender with the memory of an old pain.

"I hired on for a cattle drive up to Kansas," he explained. "When I got back, they told me she got sick and died. I didn't even get to tell her goodbye."

Tex's voice trailed off, and the room became silent. I glanced at Yancy, and his face was somber.

Tex uttered a small laugh.

"It's like they say," he said. "You never realize what you have until it's gone. She was so small and frail. In fact," he added, "Emily reminds me of her some."

Tex looked at us, smiled sadly, and leaned back on his bunk.

I now knew the reason Tex drank. I didn't know how, but I was suddenly determined to help him. I glanced at Yancy, but I couldn't tell what he was thinking.

"I'll get you some firewood and coffee," I said.

"Thanks, boss."

"And you won't leave the jail?"

"I won't," Tex declared. "You have my word."

I nodded, and Yancy and I turned and left.

CHAPTER TWENTY-NINE

"Fine pair of Texas Rangers we make," Yancy grumbled as we walked down the street. "We locked a prisoner in a jail that doesn't even work."

"I won't tell anybody if you don't," I replied.

Yancy grunted, and I pursed my lips as I looked down the street.

Emily and Little Ben were still sitting in the buggy beside the feed shop. There was no sign of her husband.

"Might as well talk to Emily now," I said, and I looked at Yancy and asked, "Want to come along?"

"Think I should?"

"Your appearance might be helpful."

"My appearance?"

"Sure," I nodded. "Way you look, it might scare some sense into her."

"I'm not sure how to take that."

"I meant it in a good way."

Yancy frowned at me, and we walked toward them. Emily spotted us, and a concerned look crossed her face.

"Hello again," I smiled as we stopped beside the buggy. "You remember my brother?"

"Of course," she flashed us a nervous smile.

"I'm sorry to bother you again, but we need to talk," I said.

"Mr. Landon, *please*," she insisted. "This will only cause trouble."

"Might," I agreed, and I looked at Little Ben and smiled. "Son, could you give us a moment?"

He looked at his mother. Emily looked anxious, but she still nodded.

"Go stand on the sidewalk and watch for your father," she told him.

89

"Yes, Ma," Little Ben said, and he bounded out of the buggy.

"You've got a good looking boy," I commented as we watched him.

"I am very proud of him," Emily replied.

"You should be," I said. I paused, and then asked, "Emily, what's your husband's name?"

"Big Ben," she said, and her face stiffened.

"He's not so big, really," I commented.

"No, but he's bigger than Little Ben."

"I reckon he is," I agreed. It was silent a moment, and I added, "Emily, we'd like to help."

"There's nothing you can do."

"Actually, there might be."

"You'd only cause trouble, and he'd take it out on us."

"I'd like to talk to Big Ben," Yancy spoke up, and his voice was dangerously soft.

Emily's eyes grew wide.

"*Talk* to him?"

"Sure."

"Talking will only make things worse," Emily replied. "He'd be furious if he found out *we* were talking."

Yancy didn't reply, and Emily continued.

"He isn't as bad as he seems," she insisted.

"Hard to be worse," I replied.

"Running a ranch is very stressful," she tried to explain. "It won't rain, and we have no money. In fact, we're stopping at the bank today to try and get another loan. That's the only way we'll make it until shipping time."

Neither Yancy nor I said anything.

"The strain gets to him sometimes. Then he drinks, gets mad, and takes it out on us," she said.

"He ain't supposed to," Yancy said.

She had no reply to that, and it was silent a moment.

"Do you love him?" I asked suddenly.

Emily was startled by the question.

90

"Love? I'm not sure I even know what that is anymore," she admitted.

"Then why'd you marry him?" Yancy asked, and he seemed genuinely interested.

"It was an arranged marriage," she explained. "I had no choice."

"You do now," I replied. "We can arrange to *un-arrange* the marriage."

"But then I'd lose Little Ben."

"He's *your* son, isn't he?" I asked.

"No, he's from a previous marriage," Emily replied. "But, I feel as if he's my own. We've grown quite close."

It fell silent as we thought on that.

"No," she said, taking advantage of the silence. "I appreciate your concerns, but we'd have no place to go, and no way to make a living. Don't you understand?"

"It'll happen again," Yancy said, his voice quiet.

"I just have to learn not to nag him," she replied.

Yancy frowned. He glanced at me and looked back at her.

"You won't change your mind?"

"No," she said. "I just can't."

Yancy's frown deepened, but neither one of us replied.

"Now *please*," she begged. "Go before Big Ben sees us."

"As you wish," Yancy said.

I nodded goodbye, and we turned and walked down the street.

CHAPTER THIRTY

We stopped in front of the general store. I glanced at Yancy, and he had a brooding look.

There was movement down the street, and we watched as Big Ben came out of the feed store. He untied the horse, stepped into the buggy, and went down to the bank. Big Ben climbed down, tied the horse to the hitching rail, spoke curtly to Emily, and went inside.

"Coop," Yancy said, his voice thoughtful.

"Yes?"

"If I asked you to do something, would you?"

"I have been all morning."

Yancy was silent a moment.

Then he said, "I want you to disable the Basset's buggy."

"What?" I was startled.

"You heard me."

"You mean like, without being seen?"

"Be better."

"How am I supposed to do that?"

"They'll probably eat lunch at the café," Yancy figured. "Be a good time to do it."

"And what would this accomplish?" I stared at Yancy.

"I need time to contemplate things before they leave town," he replied.

"Contemplate what?" I asked. "Emily doesn't want our help."

"Actually, she does, she just doesn't know it yet."

"But she said–."

"I know; I heard her."

"Then what *can* we do?"

"That's what I need to contemplate."

I studied Yancy a moment and sighed.

"We could get into trouble, Yancy," I warned.

"Not if we handle it right."

"What are we going to do, kill him?"

"Not a bad idea."

"That wouldn't help Emily," I reminded. "You heard what she said. They would be all alone with no income."

"For a while," Yancy replied. "Pretty as she is, she wouldn't stay single long."

"But she wants to stay with her husband. She even said so."

Yancy looked at me and scowled.

"We ain't gonna kill him," he said.

I was relieved to hear it.

"What then?" I asked.

"I don't know yet," Yancy admitted. "But, I'll think of something."

I took in a deep breath and sighed.

"What if I get caught? Be hard to explain."

"Just don't."

"More words of wisdom," I grumbled.

"Will you do it?"

We looked at each other a moment, but his determined look never wavered.

"Fine," I muttered. "But you really owe me."

"Thanks, Coop."

I mumbled a reply, and Yancy grinned and started to walk inside the general store. But he stopped as another thought occurred to him.

"Don't forget about Wagons," he said.

"Headed there now," I replied.

"And Carlos."

"Haven't forgot about him either."

"Thanks Coop. For everything."

I decided to use Wyatt's favorite word.

"Sure," I replied.

CHAPTER THIRTY-ONE

Moments later, I stepped up onto the porch at the jail. I thought briefly about knocking, but quickly discarded the idea.

I opened the door and marched in. The office was empty, so I shut the door and walked to the desk.

I was flooded with memories as I looked around.

This had once been our office. Back then we'd just arrived in Texas, and we were members of the Texas Police force.

A loud, irritating snore interrupted my thoughts. It came from the back where the cells were, so I walked to the doorway and looked in.

All the cells were empty, except for one. The person occupying that cell was none other than our honorable sheriff.

Wagons was stretched out on the bunk, and his hat covered his face as he slept. He still wore the same clothes from last night, and they were wrinkled and crumply looking.

I started to wake him, but stopped when a crazy notion occurred to me. And, the more I thought on it, the more I liked it.

I surveyed the jail cells. As I had hoped, Wagons had hung his gun belt in the hallway. It was on a peg beside the jail keys.

I eased over to Wagon's cell, grabbed the door, and pulled it shut. It made a soft click, and I winced. However, Wagons never ceased his snoring, and I grinned wolfishly.

I turned from the cell and grabbed the jail keys. Then, being quiet as possible, I eased down the hallway to the office, and I shut the door behind me.

I grinned briefly. Then, I walked over to the desk, opened the bottom drawer, and hid the jail keys underneath some papers. Next, I rummaged through the desk and found a pencil. I wrote a note on a piece of paper that read:

Gone for a spell. Be back this afternoon.

I read the note several times and nodded my approval. I returned the pencil to the desk, walked outside, shut the door, pinned the note in clear display, and chuckled as I walked down the street.

CHAPTER THIRTY-TWO

It was nearing noon.

At the other end of town, I spotted Big Ben coming out of the bank. He untied his horse and climbed into the buggy, and they went down the street and stopped at the café. This time, all three of them got down and went inside.

"Well, here goes," I said to myself.

I hurried to the blacksmith shop and went inside.

The blacksmith's name was Dean. He was a big man, with broad, beefy shoulders. He was always honest and friendly, and he liked us Landons.

Dean was shaping a horseshoe, and he glanced up and spotted me.

"Coop," he greeted. "What brings you here?"

"I need to borrow a pair of pliers," I replied, then added, "I think."

"Sure," he gestured with his head at a workbench. "You'll find what you need over there."

I walked over to the table. I spotted a pair of pliers, and I picked them up, handled them some, and nodded my approval.

"Thanks," I said. "I'll bring them right back."

"Sure thing, Coop."

I moved to the door, but I didn't go out. I just stood there, and Dean looked up and noticed my hesitant look.

"Is there something else?" He asked.

I frowned as I pondered how to answer that. I actually hadn't been around buggies much, and didn't know much about them.

"You know about buggies?" I asked.

"I ought to," Dean grinned. "I've worked on them enough."

"How would one go about disabling one?" I asked nonchalantly.

A confused look crossed Dean's face.

"Disabling it?"

"Sure. So it can't leave."

"You mean, like taking the wheel off?"

"That would work," I replied. "Unless there's an easier way."

"Well, it depends," Dean looked thoughtful. "What sort of buggy are we talking about?"

"Nothing fancy," I tried to look innocent. "Just a plain, one seat buggy with two wheels."

"Like the Basset's buggy?"

"*Exactly* like that."

"Nothing to it," Dean said. "Those are simple made buggies. Only thing holding the wheel on is a single nut on a bolt. Unscrew it, and the wheel slides right off."

"That's it?" I smiled my pleasure.

"Sure. What's this about?"

"Texas Ranger business," I said sternly. Then, as a thought occurred to me, I pulled out the pliers and showed them to Dean. "Would these get the job done?"

"Should, long as it's not too rusty. If it is you'll need some grease."

"Appreciate the information."

"Glad I could help."

I nodded, pocketed the pliers, and eased out into the street.

CHAPTER THIRTY-THREE

Acting as nonchalant as possible, I moseyed over to the Bassett's buggy.

I came up beside the horse and spoke soothing words, but he seemed disinterested. I patted him on the back, and, using him as a shield, I surveyed the street.

I didn't see anybody, and I grunted my satisfaction.

I moved to the wheel and studied it. I found the bolt Dean had mentioned, and I also spotted the nut. Luckily it wasn't rusty, and I had no trouble unscrewing it with the pliers.

I dropped the nut in my shirt pocket, pocketed the pliers, and tugged on the wheel.

Even though it was loose, I couldn't budge it, and I frowned at my misfortune. In order to get the wheel off, the buggy needed to be lifted. The problem was I couldn't lift *and* pull at the same time.

I glanced around, hoping to see something I could use for leverage. I didn't see anything, and I was standing there trying to think when I heard a noise from behind. I spun around and spotted Wyatt.

He was standing in the alley, watching me with a puzzled expression.

"Wyatt," I hissed. "What are you doing here?"

"Looking for you," he said.

"Well, you accomplished that."

"You busy?"

"Only a little."

"What are you doing to that buggy?"

He walked towards me, but I leaned over the wheel so he couldn't see.

"Nothing much," I tried to look innocent. "Dean and I were discussing buggies, and I was interested in something."

Wyatt looked at me oddly, but didn't say anything.

"What's going on?" I tried to change the subject.

An earnest look crossed Wyatt's face. He stood there a moment, collecting his thoughts, while I glanced up and down the street.

"I wanted to say I was sorry," Wyatt finally said. "I was wrong this morning."

I was surprised by his confession, and I stared at him a moment.

"I appreciate you saying that," I said, my voice soft.

"I was mad, and I just didn't think."

"It happens," I replied. "We'll just forget about it and move on."

"Thanks," Wyatt grinned at me.

"Don't mention it," I said. "In fact, let's not mention anything about this."

"What do you mean?"

"Oh, nothing."

Wyatt nodded, and his face turned serious.

"Tex is still my friend," he declared. "Nothing's going to change that."

"I can understand that," I said. "I like Tex too."

A thought occurred to me as soon as I spoke Tex's name, and I grunted softly.

"Does he still have to go to prison?" Wyatt asked, interrupting my thoughts.

"What?" I looked back at Wyatt. "Who?"

"Tex," Wyatt looked strangely at me.

"Oh," I tried to recover. "I'm not sure, Wyatt. But Tex needs help, and prison might be the best thing for him."

Wyatt nodded, but he didn't look convinced.

"We'll talk more later," I said, then urged, "Why don't you go apologize to Josie? She'd like that."

"Think I should?"

"Yes."

"Now?"

"Yes, *now.*"

"All right," Wyatt gave me a cheerful grin. "I'll do that."

"That's a fine idea," I prompted.

"I'll see you later then?"

"Yes, *later.*"

Wyatt nodded and eased down the street.

I stood there and watched him. Some other folks passed by, and I smiled and nodded at them.

As soon as everyone was gone, I hurried across the street to the Texas Ranger station. I entered the alley and stopped underneath Tex's window.

"Tex!" I hissed.

There was movement, and Tex's face appeared from the edge of his bunk.

"Yes, boss?"

"Get out here. *Quick!*"

Tex looked hesitant.

"Is this a test or something?"

"Move it!" I replied tersely. "*Now!*"

"Yes sir, boss."

He jumped off the bunk, and moments later he met me in the alley.

"What's going on, boss?" He asked.

"Follow me," I gestured.

I hurried across the street, and nobody saw us as we approached the buggy.

"Pick up this corner here," I gestured.

"What for, boss?"

"Just do it!"

"Yes sir, boss."

He picked up the buggy with ease, and I slid the wheel off.

"Now set it down!" I hissed.

He did, and the axle went all the way to the ground. I leaned the wheel against the buggy, and then I glanced up and down the street. Nobody had seen us, and I grunted my satisfaction.

"Now go back to jail," I told Tex. "I'll explain later."

"Yes sir, boss."

I waited while Tex walked across the street, and then I hurried away from the scene of the crime.

CHAPTER THIRTY-FOUR

I returned to the blacksmith shop, and Dean glanced up from his work as I entered.

"That didn't take long," he remarked he watched me return the pliers to the workbench.

I ignored Dean's comment as I turned to him.

"You'll probably have another customer *real* soon," I announced.

"Oh?" Dean looked interested. "Who?"

"Big Ben Basset."

"Big Ben? He was already here."

"Well, he'll be back."

"What for?"

I reached into my pocket, pulled out the nut, and handed it over.

"His buggy is missing this," I explained.

"You disabled Big Ben's buggy?" Dean's eyes grew wide.

"More or less."

"I don't understand."

"You aren't supposed to."

"And you want me to fix it?" Dean asked, and he watched my face closely.

"Actually, we don't want Big Ben leaving town for a while," I instructed.

"We?"

"Me and Yancy."

Dean nodded slowly as understanding began to dawn on him.

"You want me to stall him."

"It would be appreciated."

"What's this about?"

"Can't say too much," I replied.

"More Texas Ranger business?"

"Exactly."

Dean nodded and pinched his face in thought.

"Doesn't surprise me if Big Ben's in trouble with the law," he commented. "He has a temper, and I don't like the way he treats his family. I've seen things."

"I have a feeling that temper's about to flare up."

"Let it. He doesn't worry me none."

"So you'll help us?" I asked.

"I'll do what I can."

"'Preciate it," I replied.

Dean nodded, and I turned toward the door.

CHAPTER THIRTY-FIVE

It was just past noon. Yancy and I were at the Texas Ranger station, thinking of lunch, and fearing that Josie might bring us some.

Earlier, Yancy had brought Tex some firewood and coffee. Tex already had a fire going and had also made a pot of coffee.

I hadn't had time to gather Tex's supplies, and I was surprised that Yancy had remembered. I wondered briefly if Yancy was changing his mind about Tex, but his face revealed nothing.

"Saw the buggy," Yancy commented as he poured a cup of coffee. He poured in his usual three spoonfuls of sugar and stirred.

"Tex helped," I said.

Yancy nodded and took a swig. His good eye grew wide, and a surprised grunt escaped his lips.

"Good coffee," he remarked, obviously impressed.

"I have a special way of making it," Tex explained. "You like it?"

"I sure do!"

"I always thought life was too short for bad coffee," Tex declared.

"My thoughts exactly," Yancy agreed.

Tex nodded emphatically, and Yancy scrunched his face in thought as he studied Tex.

It was silent for a few seconds, and then I heard Yancy grunt softly in admiration. He and Tex now had something in common, and at that exact moment, I saw a change in Yancy's eyes.

Or, I should say *eye*.

I smiled and walked to the wood stove. I poured a cup, took a swig, and grunted my approval.

"It is good coffee," I remarked.

Yancy nodded again, and I took another swig as I walked over to the window. Yancy and Tex joined me, and we watched the café in anticipation.

"Whose buggy was that?" Tex asked.

"Big Ben's," I explained, and Tex grunted in surprise.

A few minutes passed, and the Basetts came out of the café. Big Ben led the way, and Emily followed, holding Little Ben's hand.

We didn't want to be seen, so we hid behind the wood frame of the window as best as we could.

Big Ben stopped abruptly. He stared at the wheel in disbelief, and then he walked forward. He stopped beside the buggy and peered down, his hands on his hips.

After a moment, Big Ben straightened and circled the buggy. He glanced up and down the street, and then looked back at the wheel.

Emily came up beside him. She said something, but Big Ben made an abrupt motion to be quiet.

Emily tried again, and he turned sharply towards her. He shouted something and raised his hand.

He managed to stop just before he hit her. Emily shrank back, and Big Ben just stood there, glaring at her. Then he turned abruptly toward the buggy and started unhitching the horse. After he finished, Big Ben walked briskly toward the blacksmith shop.

Emily called after him, but he ignored her. She stood there a moment, unsure what to do, and then she tugged on Little Ben's hand and trailed after him.

"Like I said," Tex said softly. "He doesn't deserve her."

"I'd say so," Yancy agreed.

"Now what?" I looked at Yancy. "I have an understanding with Dean, but he can't keep them in town forever."

"Let's see what happens," Yancy replied.

I didn't understand that remark, but Yancy spoke again before I could reply.

"You hungry?"

"Always," I replied.

"Let's eat at the café."

"But Josie might be bringing something," I reminded.

Yancy looked at me, and his face was without expression.

"Let's eat at the café," he repeated.

I smiled, nodded, and used the word for the day again.

"Sure," I said.

Yancy turned to Tex.

"And you –."

"I know," Tex interrupted. "Get back in my cell."

"No," Yancy replied. "You're coming with us."

Tex was surprised by the offer, as was I.

"I thought I was a prisoner," he said.

"You are," Yancy replied. "But, this'll save us the trouble of fetching you something."

Tex nodded his acceptance, and he turned to the stove and set the pot of coffee to the side. Meanwhile, Yancy and I cleaned our cups, and then we left the office.

"You talk to Wagons?" Yancy asked me as we crossed the street.

"More or less," I replied.

"What does that mean?"

"Means he's been taken care of."

Yancy raised an eyebrow.

"How did you manage that?"

I started to reply, but stopped.

"It's probably best if you don't know," I said.

"Know what?"

"Exactly," I said.

CHAPTER THIRTY-SIX

A few minutes later, we were seated at a corner table in the café. We ordered coffee, beans, and steak.

The café was a long, narrow room. It wasn't fancy, but the food was good, and that's all that mattered.

"You talk to Carlos yet?" Yancy asked while we waited for our food.

"Not sure if you've noticed, but I've been a little busy," I replied.

"I've noticed. Just reminding you."

"I'll get around to it."

"You also need to stop by the general store," Yancy informed.

"What for?" I raised an eyebrow.

"To pick out some new clothes," Yancy explained. "I already paid; they're expecting you."

"I ain't the one getting married," I protested.

"But you'll be my best man," Yancy informed.

"I am?" I asked, startled.

"Who else would I get?" Yancy scowled at me.

"Well," I said, deeply moved. "I appreciate that."

"And you also need another bath and shave," Yancy suggested.

"I'll fit it in somehow."

The waiter brought our food over, and we tore into our steaks. Tex seemed especially hungry, and it didn't take us long to wolf our food down.

I was taking my last bite when there was a commotion at the door. I heard a rustling of skirts, and I looked up and spotted Emily and Little Ben.

Emily was crying. Her eyes were red, and her cheeks wet. She hurried toward us, and she dragged Little Ben along.

I glanced sideways at Tex. He was watching her closely, and his face went rigid.

Emily stopped in front of us, and it was silent while we looked at her.

"Emily," I finally greeted.

"I need your help," she replied, and her voice trembled.

"What's wrong?" I asked.

"Big Ben just hit me. Again."

There was a fresh, red mark on her face. Tex saw it too, and he clenched his fists.

"Why'd he do that?" I asked.

"Something happened to our buggy," Emily explained. "Big Ben is real upset about it. I tried to calm him when he returned from the blacksmith, but he just exploded."

I glanced at Yancy, expecting him to rush to her aid, but instead he just sat there, looking thoughtful.

"I thought you didn't want our help," Yancy reminded.

Tex shot Yancy an ugly look, but Yancy ignored him.

"I – I just don't know what to do," Emily stammered, and more tears streamed down her face.

Yancy nodded. He started to reply, but paused when there was movement at the door. We all looked, and Big Ben burst in.

"Here comes your husband," Yancy said, his voice flat.

CHAPTER THIRTY-SEVEN

Like Emily said; Big Ben looked upset.

He glanced around the room, and his eyes had a crazed look. He spotted us, didn't like what he saw, scowled, and walked over. Meanwhile, Emily and Little Ben hurried around the table, putting us between them and Big Ben.

I expected Yancy to stand to meet Big Ben, but he didn't. Instead, he just sat there with an expressionless face. Tex however, glared at Big Ben, and his knuckles turned white as he clenched his fists even tighter.

Big Ben stopped at our table. He looked at Emily, and then at us.

"You the Landons?" He demanded.

I started to reply, but Yancy surprised me once again.

"We are," Yancy said, his voice pleasant.

"Been looking for you," he said.

"Looks like you found us," Yancy replied.

"My name's –."

"We know who you are," Yancy interrupted.

Big Ben hesitated, blinked, and then continued.

"I was told there's a sheriff in this town, but I can't locate him. The blacksmith suggested I find you."

"What do you need?" Yancy asked.

"Somebody sabotaged my buggy!" Big Ben blurted, and his voice shook with anger.

"You don't say," Yancy said, unmoved.

"I want *you* to find who's responsible."

Yancy glanced across the table at me, and then looked back at Big Ben.

"Shouldn't be too hard," he said. Then, in the same breath, Yancy asked, "What happened to your wife's face?"

Big Ben was startled by the question.

"What?" He stared at Yancy.

"I think you heard me."

109

It was silent for several seconds as Big Ben thought on that. He must have chose to ignore the question, because he looked past us at Emily.

"Get down to the blacksmith shop," he said. "Now."

Emily swallowed and shook her head.

"No," she said. "We won't do that. Not anymore."

"I won't ask you again, woman."

Tex stood abruptly. His eyes glowed, and he was so mad his arms shook. Yancy meanwhile, remained seated, taking everything in calmly.

Big Ben stared at Tex. It was obvious Tex's size startled him, and he took a small step backwards. But his pride was at stake, and he couldn't let it go.

"This is none of your business," he said, then added, "Any of you."

"Suppose I make it my business," Tex growled.

"You can't do that," Big Ben tried again.

Tex glanced at Yancy.

"You gonna stop me if there's trouble?" He asked.

"Still pondering that," Yancy replied.

Tex grunted and looked at Emily.

"What do you want me to do, ma'am?"

"Do?" Emily looked confused.

"I'll do anything you want."

"Oh my! I don't want you to do anything!"

Tex frowned his disappointment. He remained standing, and he looked back at Big Ben and narrowed his eyes.

"I don't know what Emily's been saying, but she lies all the time," Big Ben said, taking advantage of the silence.

Nobody said anything, and the silence grew tense.

"This is between me and my wife," Big Ben tried again. "None of you have the right to interfere."

Again, our response was silence.

Big Ben scowled and looked at his wife.

"Let's go," he said, more quietly this time.

Emily shook her head.

110

"You won't come with me?" He stared at her.

"No, Ben. I just can't."

Big Ben muttered under his breath. He scowled at Emily, and then looked at Little Ben.

"Fine," he grunted. "You can stay here for all I care. Let's go, son."

Little Ben shook his head and gripped Emily's hand.

Big Ben glared at him.

"You too, eh?"

Little Ben nodded.

"Well, that's just fine," Big Ben muttered.

He started to leave, but Yancy stopped him.

"While we have a moment," Yancy said.

"What?" Big Ben glared at him.

"Your cows are having difficulties staying home."

"Who told you that?"

Yancy ignored the question.

"You'd better figure something out. You might lose your cows for good if you can't keep 'em from straying."

"Lose them?" Big Ben frowned.

"Sure. Your neighbors might decide to make your cows their own. After all, they're eating their grass."

"But that ain't right."

"Neither is letting them drift and not doing anything about it."

"It doesn't matter," Big Ben objected. "It's free range."

"You are mistaken," Yancy said, and there was a warning in his voice not to challenge it.

Big Ben was mad. He stared at Yancy, and Yancy stared back. Several seconds passed, and then Big Ben snorted.

He spun around and walked briskly toward the door. He slammed open the batwing doors on his way out, and they swung behind him.

Emily started crying again, and Tex turned to comfort her.

"Don't cry, ma'am," he said, his voice suddenly gentle. "It'll be all right."

Emily sobbed harder.

I looked at Yancy. He was just sitting there with a calm expression, watching Tex and looking thoughtful.

CHAPTER THIRTY-EIGHT

We left the café a few minutes later. Yancy took Tex back to jail, and I walked with Emily up the street. Little Ben trailed along behind us.

Tears still streamed down Emily's face. She kept wiping her cheeks with her hand and sniffling.

"I'm so embarrassed," she finally said.

"No need to be," I replied. "Wasn't your fault."

She uttered a little half-laugh.

"And it was all for nothing," she said.

"How's that?" I asked, confused.

"You do realize we have to go back. We have no choice."

"Actually, I didn't realize that."

"We don't even have a place to sleep tonight."

"I'll get you a room at the hotel," I offered.

"But I can't pay."

"Won't have to."

"Why not?" She stopped and looked at me.

"Yancy and I *do* have some clout in this town," I told her.

Surprise showed in her face.

"You'd do that for me?"

"Yes."

"Why?"

I shrugged as we started walking again.

"It's what we do," I said.

"For how long?" Emily pressed.

"How long what?" I asked, confused.

"How long can I stay at the hotel?"

"Long as you need," I replied.

More tears dribbled down her face as she thought on that.

"I can't thank you enough."

"I know. Don't even try."

"Why are you being so kind to us? You don't have to be."

"Yancy and I take turns," I replied. "Today's my day."

She smiled at that, and I smiled with her. Then I gestured up the street.

"Why don't I take you up to our house," I suggested. "Josie's had a rough day, and you'd be a welcome distraction."

"She has?" Concern filled her face.

"Not quite as rough as yours," I replied.

"I don't mind talking to her. I enjoy it. I could use the distraction myself."

"Then let's go," I urged.

CHAPTER THIRTY-NINE

I escorted Emily and Little Ben to our house. Wyatt was there too, and he and Josie seemed to be having an interesting conversation.

I studied them both, but neither of their faces revealed anything. However, the mood didn't seem as tense as before.

Josie gasped when she saw Emily's face. She glanced at me for an explanation, but I shook my head slightly. Josie understood to change the subject, and she ushered Emily into the kitchen.

Wyatt sensed that something was wrong. He approached Little Ben, and it didn't take them long to start talking.

I caught Wyatt's eye and nodded my appreciation. He returned the nod, and I turned and left.

I spotted a wagon coming into town as I walked down the street. I squinted at it and recognized Tussle and Jessica.

Her face was glowing with happiness. She spotted me, and she grinned and waved. Tussle meanwhile, looked the same as he always did. He displayed a tight frown and looked irritable.

"Hello, Coop!" Jessica called out as they stopped beside me.

"Why Miss Jessica, you look lovely," I said pleasantly.

"Thank you," she blushed.

I looked at Tussle.

"How are you, Tussle?"

"Bursting with joy," he said flatly.

"Must be the inward sort you can't see," I jested.

Tussle grunted in response and remained silent.

"How is Yancy today?" Jessica spoke up.

I hesitated while I pondered how to answer that.

"Not quite the same as yesterday," I finally said.

She grinned with pleasure.

"I should hope not! He's getting married!"

"It's not that," I replied. "We've had trouble."

"Oh?" Jessica raised an eyebrow. "What sort of trouble?"

"Well, these bad guys rode in…"

"Bad guys?"

"Yes, ma'am."

"How bad, exactly?"

"We haven't decided yet."

Jessica bit her lower lip as she thought on that.

"Are they causing problems?"

"Not yet, but they could."

"I don't like this."

"Don't worry," I tried to sound cheerful. "Yancy and I will take care of them."

"And where is Yancy?" She wanted to know.

"Probably at the Texas Ranger station," I replied. "Taking care of a prisoner."

"What prisoner?"

"We had trouble last night too," I explained. I looked at Tussle and added, "It's Tex."

Tussle didn't seem surprised.

"What'd he do this time?" He asked.

"Plenty," I said, and then explained.

A concerned look crossed Jessica's face.

"Tex hit Yancy?"

"Sure did. And *then* hurled him across the room."

"Oh my!" Her eyes grew wide. "You're sure Yancy is all right?"

"Oh, he's just *fine*," I waved a hand at her.

Jessica looked upset.

"Well! I think Tex should go to prison!"

"It's possible," I replied. "It just depends."

"Depends on what?"

I grinned briefly.

"Might depend on coffee."

"Coffee?" Jessica was confused.

"Sort of a private joke," I explained.

Jessica frowned. However, before she could reply, Tussle spoke up.

"I'd hate to lose Tex," he remarked. "He's a good hand."

I nodded my agreement and changed the subject.

"Why don't you two go on up to the house," I offered. "Josie's expecting you, and you can change into your wedding dress there."

Excitement filled Jessica's face as her thoughts returned to the wedding.

"Thank you, Coop," she said. "I was hoping I could. I want to include Josie as much as I can."

"I appreciate that," I said.

"Of course," Jessica replied. "We're sister-in-laws now."

"Sure are," I agreed. I glanced at the sun, and added, "Well, time is running short. I'd best get busy."

Jessica nodded, and I started to walk away.

"Coop," Jessica stopped me.

"Yes?" I looked back at her.

"Take care of Yancy. I'm too young to be a widow."

"Yes, ma'am," I smiled.

CHAPTER FORTY

I walked on down the street. I spotted Dean coming from the café, and he gestured at me.

"How are things with Big Ben?" Dean asked as we met.

"Not sure, really," I replied.

"I just looked at his buggy. He's very upset."

"I would agree with that assessment," I smiled.

"I won't be able to stall him long. He knows about buggies, and it's an easy fix."

"Go ahead and repair it," I replied. "We accomplished something."

He nodded, and another thought occurred to me.

"There's something else," I said.

"Oh?"

"I figure someone else ought to know, just in case."

"Know what?"

I scrunched my face in thought.

"Not sure how to explain it," I admitted.

"Just say it," Dean encouraged.

I took in a deep breath and exhaled.

"We've, ah, had all sorts of troubles today," I tried to explain.

"I've noticed."

"Might be more trouble coming."

"Oh?"

"If something were to happen to me, you'll need to go to the jail," I continued.

"The Sheriff's office?"

"That is correct," I nodded. "You'll find jail keys in the bottom drawer of the desk, underneath some papers."

"What are they doing there?" Dean watched my face closely.

"Texas Ranger business," I replied.

Dean frowned at that.

"You don't want me to know?"

"Not particularly."

"All right," Dean nodded slowly. "*If* something were to happen, what am I supposed to do with these jail keys?"

"Walk back to the jail cells," I instructed, "and you'll understand."

"All right, Coop. Whatever you say."

"And if nothing bad does happen, just forget we had this conversation."

"What conversation?" Dean smiled wryly.

I smiled with him.

"Thanks, Dean. I appreciate your help."

Dean nodded and studied me a moment.

Then he asked, "Do you Landons ever experience normal, peaceful days?"

"Not so much."

"Sorta figured that," Dean replied.

CHAPTER FORTY-ONE

I still hadn't figured out what to say to Carlos. So, instead of the saloon, I headed for the hotel.

I arranged for a room for Emily, and then I went to the general store. I picked out a new set of clothes, and the lady helping me wrapped them up in some brown paper. I stuck the package under my arm, walked out into the street, and headed for the Texas Ranger station.

I was startled when I spotted Tex. He had just stepped out the front door, and he was walking across the street with a look of determination.

I quickened my steps. I started to call out, but stopped myself when I spotted Yancy. He was standing at the window, watching Tex through the opening.

Yancy's focus was so intense, he hardly noticed as I walked through the open doorway. I placed my package on the desk and joined him at the window.

"What's going on?" I demanded, then asked, "Where's Tex going?"

"On an errand," Yancy replied, his eyes still on Tex.

"I don't understand," I said.

Yancy didn't reply, and it was silent for several seconds.

A speech for Yancy is if he grunts twice, so I was surprised when he started talking.

"Tex and I had a long, good talk. We even drank some more coffee."

"Did Tex make it?" I asked.

"He sure did."

I smiled briefly.

"What did you talk about?" I asked.

"We discussed his late wife, his drinking problem, and some other things," Yancy said, then added, "You know, Tex is a good fella after you get to know him."

"He is likeable," I agreed.

120

"We also reached an agreement."

"Oh?" I was interested.

Yancy paused a moment.

Then he said, "Tex has agreed to quit drinking. For good."

I narrowed my eyes in suspicion.

"Sounds nice," I said.

"I thought so."

"I admire his intentions, but what if he *can't* stop?" I argued.

"I think he can."

"Yes, but suppose he has a weak moment, gets drunk, and busts up the saloon again?"

"Then we'll have to deal with it."

I studied Yancy and frowned.

"You seem confident."

"I told you. We had a good discussion."

"And that's good enough for you?"

"It is."

"Just like that?"

"Just like that."

I thought on that a moment.

"So, you ain't mad at him anymore?" I finally asked.

"Aw, that was this morning."

"Before he made you coffee," I said wryly.

"Well, a lot's happened since then," Yancy ignored my sarcasm.

I nodded, then asked, "So, Tex isn't going to jail?"

"Not for now."

"And that's the agreement?"

"Not entirely."

"What else?"

"Just wait and see."

I frowned at that, and Yancy glanced at me and noticed my expression.

"I thought you'd be happy about this," he said.

"I am, mostly," I replied.

"What's wrong?"

"There's other things to consider."

"Such as?"

"Wyatt," I reminded.

"Oh," Yancy said. He thought on that, then added, "Well, that's your department. Anything you want to add to the agreement is fine by me."

"I'll think on it," I replied.

"'Course, if Tex ain't drinking, I don't see any reason for Wyatt not to be around him."

"I'll think on it," I repeated.

Yancy nodded, and we both looked out the window.

A few seconds passed, and an intriguing thought occurred to me. I suppressed a grin and managed to keep an expressionless face.

"So, this was a verbal agreement between you and Tex," I said.

"We didn't take the time to write up a contract, if that's what you mean."

"You remember what Pa said about verbal agreements," I commented.

Yancy looked at me and frowned.

"No, I don't recall."

"Any verbal agreement should end with a firm handshake," I declared.

"Pa said that?"

"Don't you remember?"

"No."

"Well, he did. Several times actually."

Yancy took in a deep breath and sighed.

"*If* I agree to shake on it, will you *please* hush up?"

"It's the proper thing to do," I declared.

"Fine."

I grinned, and the conversation came to an end.

CHAPTER FORTY-TWO

The room filled with silence. We just stood at the window, watching Tex.

He was across the street, loitering about on the sidewalk. Finally, he sat on a hitching rail. He kept looking up and down the street, as if he was looking for someone.

I had questions, but Yancy was done talking. His eyes never left Tex, and he twitched his jaw in silent anticipation.

Several minutes passed, and the tension built. And then, Tex jumped to his feet. He clenched his fists, and an ugly snarl crossed his face.

I looked down the street and spotted Big Ben.

He was still upset. He was walking towards Tex, and his movements were curt and jerky.

Tex just stood there, waiting. But then Big Ben spotted him, and he came to an abrupt stop.

They stared at each other a moment. Neither one was armed, and I figured that was a good thing.

Big Ben turned and left the sidewalk. His intent was to walk around Tex, but Tex walked out into the street and blocked him.

Big Ben halted, and his jaw muscles rippled as he stared at Tex. Tex returned the stare, his face mean and hard.

Big Ben didn't like it. He turned abruptly and moved back toward the sidewalk, but so did Tex.

He stopped again. He took several steps backward, but Tex moved with him. Then Big Ben stopped moving, and they stood there face to face.

Big Ben said something. Tex didn't react, and they stood there some more.

Suddenly, Tex moved swiftly. He jumped forward, swung his fist, and connected a staggering blow to Big Ben's jaw.

Big Ben staggered backwards. He tried to hit back, but Tex blocked his feeble attempt with his forearm. Then Tex swung again and connected with Big Ben's nose. It was a solid blow, and Big Ben hollered in pain and collapsed.

Tex jumped on top of him, and he peppered Big Ben's face with short, powerful blows.

Big Ben tried to fend him off, but he was helpless. Then he just lay there, his mouth open, as Tex continued his assault.

By now blood covered Big Ben's face, and I could almost hear bones crunching under Tex's powerful blows.

"He's gonna kill him!" I exclaimed, and moved toward the door.

Yancy reached out and grabbed my arm.

"He won't go that far," he said.

I scowled at Yancy and looked out the window.

Tex finally stopped swinging, and Big Ben just lay there in complete defeat. Tex reached down, grabbed a handful of hair, and pulled his face up within inches of his own. He said something in his ear, and then he let go. Big Ben's head hit the ground as Tex stood.

Tex looked across the street at us. He nodded, and Yancy returned the nod. Then Tex turned and walked away, leaving Big Ben lying in the street.

CHAPTER FORTY-THREE

I turned from the window and looked at Yancy.

He displayed a crooked grin. His good eye was twinkling, and he made no attempt to hide his pleasure.

"*That* was your arrangement," I accused.

Yancy looked at me.

"Is that a question?" He asked.

"Might as well be."

"I have no reply."

I frowned at Yancy, but he ignored me as he walked over to the stove. He poured himself a cup of coffee, poured in his sugar, stirred, took a deep swig, and heaved a satisfied sigh.

I joined him at the stove. I also poured a cup and tried to look stern.

"That wasn't exactly legal, Yancy," I said.

"Perhaps not," Yancy agreed. "But effective."

"How so?"

"Big Ben knows how it feels now. If he ever hits Emily again, Tex will pay him another visit."

"Is that what Tex told him?"

"More or less."

I scrunched my face as I thought on that. And, I had to admit, the more I considered it, the more I liked it.

"The ol' eye for an eye concept," I said.

"More like tooth for tooth," Yancy corrected.

I chuckled and shook my head.

"I'd say Tex got his point across."

"Sure did," Yancy agreed. He felt his jaw, winced, and said, "Tex can hit hard."

"You know from experience."

"I sure do."

I grinned at that.

"Sure are a lot of black eyes going around," I commented.

Yancy looked at me.

"You feeling left out?"

"Yes, but in a good way."

"I could help with that," Yancy offered.

"I wouldn't want to hurt your hand," I replied. Then, to myself, I thought, *least not until you and Tex shake hands.*

CHAPTER FORTY-FOUR

From time to time we glanced out at Big Ben, but he didn't move. He just lay on his back, his arms and legs stretched out, and his face turned up toward the sky with his mouth open.

We couldn't leave him like that, but we also didn't want to help him. We decided to wait it out.

Dean came strolling up the street a few minutes later. He spotted Big Ben and jumped in surprise. He hurried over and peered down, and then frowned when he recognized him.

Dean turned and hurried toward us. He came through the open doorway, and a surprised look crossed his face when he spotted us at the window.

"Big Ben's in the street," Dean said, stating the obvious.

"We see that," I nodded.

"What happened to him?"

I looked at Dean a moment, then said, "Texas Ranger business."

"Oh," Dean replied, then added, "Looks like he took a beating."

"Does, don't it," I agreed.

"His buggy is ready."

"Don't think he cares so much about that now," I said.

Dean nodded slowly. He looked at Yancy, and then back at me.

"Well," he said after a time. "Got some work to do. See you boys later."

"Sure thing," I said.

Dean walked back outside. He glanced at Big Ben once more, and then turned and walked up the street.

"Dean's a good fella," I commented as we watched him disappear inside the blacksmith shop.

"Seems like," Yancy agreed.

"Loyal, does what you ask, and keeps his mouth shut," I declared.

"Good traits to have," Yancy replied. "I try to be that way myself."

"You need to work on keeping your mouth shut," I jested.

"Me?" Yancy looked startled.

"You've been talking non-stop since yesterday," I pointed out.

Yancy grunted at that, but didn't reply.

CHAPTER FORTY-FIVE

A half hour passed, and Big Ben finally came to his senses.

He uttered several loud groans that sounded more like a pig dying. Then he rolled over, got up on his knees, and shook his head. He climbed to his feet, staggered some, but stayed upright.

Holding his head, he walked slowly down the street. He was headed straight for the church, but he veered sideways just before reaching there and disappeared inside the saloon.

"Thought for a second he was headed to see the pastor," I commented.

"He needs to," Yancy grunted.

"Probably plans on drowning his sorrows with whiskey instead," I assumed.

"I'd say so."

"Looks like he hasn't learned anything then."

"Well, he *did* learn how hard Tex can hit," Yancy reminded.

"Something you two have in common," I grinned.

Yancy frowned at me, and he finished his cup of coffee with one swig.

"I'm headed for the bathhouse," he said, changing the subject. "Don't forget to take one yourself."

"I'll meet you there after I talk to Carlos," I replied.

Yancy grunted in surprise.

"You haven't tended to that yet?"

"Been a little busy," I replied.

"It's midafternoon."

"You want to handle it?" I offered.

"No, no. You're doing just fine."

"Thought so," I said.

We tended to our cups. I grabbed my rifle, and we walked outside.

"Enjoy your bath," I said.

"Enjoy your visit with Carlos," Yancy replied.

I grunted, and we walked in separate directions.

CHAPTER FORTY-SIX

The Mexicans' horses were still tied to the hitching rails. I stepped up onto the porch, gathered my thoughts, and pushed through the batwing doors. I allowed my eyes to adjust and took a careful look around.

All the attention inside was directed at Big Ben. He sat at a table in the middle of the room, and blood dribbled down his face and dripped onto the table. Bart had just given him a bottle of whiskey, and he grimaced as he took a swig.

Carlos and his companions were still seated in the corner. They were drinking whiskey, and their faces sharpened when they saw me.

Holding my rifle with the barrel pointed at the floor, I walked slowly down the bar. I passed by Big Ben, but he ignored me.

I stopped in front of Carlos.

He and his companions were watching me without expression, and I returned the look. Finally, I coughed and cleared my throat, and the noise seemed loud in the quiet room.

"Came here to talk to you fellas," I announced.

"Yancy?" Carlos inquired.

"He's not coming."

A disgruntled grunt escaped his lips.

"I'll thank him, if you want," I offered.

Confusion showed in Carlos' face.

"For what?"

"If Yancy came down here, he'd kill you," I said matter-of-factly.

Carlos snorted at that.

"And if he didn't, then I would," I continued, then asked, "You have much family?"

I was changing subjects too fast for Carlos, and it took several seconds for him to reply.

"Some."

"So do we," I replied. "And, they can all handle a gun. *If something were to happen to us, they'd all come looking for you.*"

Carlos snorted again.

I waited for a reply, but there was none. Carlos just stared at me, his face dark.

"For your own good, you need to forget about your little grudge," I suggested. "If you don't, your family is only going to suffer more."

"Yancy killed my cousin," Carlos said plainly.

"He did, in the line of duty," I reminded. "It wasn't personal."

Carlos didn't reply, and a heavy silence filled the room.

Then, Carlos said, "Yancy will not come?"

"That is correct," I said. "So, you boys had best clear out."

Carlos had no reply to that; he just stared at me.

"That's all I have to say," I said. "I'll be leaving now."

Again, there was no reply. They just watched me, and I nodded at them.

I started to turn toward the door, but decided against it. Instead, I kept a watchful eye on them as I backed up.

I reached the door. I started to back out, but stopped when another thought occurred to me.

I looked at Big Ben, and he was watching me with a sour expression.

"Almost forgot," I said. "Your buggy is ready."

Big Ben showed no reaction. I smiled at him, and then eased out onto the sidewalk.

CHAPTER FORTY-SEVEN

I returned to the Texas Ranger station, collected my new clothes, and went to the bathhouse.

A Chinaman poured me a bath. I undressed and eased in, and the warmth felt good. I exhaled and relaxed as I leaned back.

Yancy had just finished his bath, and he was seated in a barber's chair with a towel wrapped around him. He was leaned back, and another Chinaman was attempting to shave him.

"How'd it go?" Yancy asked.

"I actually think it worked," I remarked.

"So they're leaving?"

"They didn't say, exactly."

"But you don't think they'll cause trouble?"

"I got the point across that you're a busy man."

Yancy gave a satisfied grunt, and after that we didn't say much. I enjoyed my bath, and Yancy suffered through his shave.

I shaved myself after my bath. Then we crawled into our new clothes, and Yancy tried to grin as he buttoned his shirt.

"How do I look?" He asked.

I studied him a moment.

His face was still swollen, and the bruises were even darker. However, the rest of him looked presentable.

"You're about as good as it's going to get," I said.

"Thanks," Yancy grunted.

"Anytime," I replied.

CHAPTER FORTY-EIGHT

We strapped on our gun belts. I grabbed my rifle, and we eased out onto the street.

We walked to the Texas Ranger station. Yancy pulled out his watch and glanced at it, and he smiled as he pocketed it.

"We've got an hour," he said, then asked, "Want some coffee?"

I stared at him.

"More coffee?" I objected. "After today, I won't sleep for a week!"

"But it's my wedding day," Yancy reminded.

"Might as well then," I shrugged.

Yancy smiled. He stirred the coals, and it didn't take him long to make a pot. He poured us both a cup, and he poured three spoonfuls of sugar in his and stirred. Then we took a swig and sighed.

"Well, looks like everything is going to work out," Yancy commented.

As soon as he said that, gunshots erupted down the street. They were loud and unexpected, and Yancy spilled coffee down the front of his shirt.

Yancy scowled and started fanning his front while I moved to the window and looked out.

"What's going on out there?" Yancy asked.

"Not sure," I replied. "I think the shots came from the saloon."

My suspicions were confirmed when Bart hurried outside and ran up the street. I gestured at him through the opening of the window, and he changed directions toward us.

"What's going on?" I asked as he burst through the doorway.

"Those Mexicans just killed Big Ben!" Bart announced.

Yancy and I were startled.

"Why'd they do that?" I asked.

Bart took several deep breaths before he replied.

"After you left, the Mexicans huddled together and talked things over," he explained. "They didn't look very pleased."

"Don't imagine they were," I replied.

"Big Ben kept drinking whiskey," Bart continued. "He started getting ugly, yelling at everybody in the room. Finally, Carlos stood and walked over to his table."

"What'd he say?" I asked.

"Nothing. He just stood there and looked at him. Big Ben asked what he wanted, but Carlos didn't reply. Then Big Ben cursed at him."

"And Carlos got upset?" I figured.

"No, Carlos just grinned," he explained. "Without a word, he drew his gun and shot Big Ben. Shot him twice. Then he went back to their table. As he sat down I heard him say, 'Yancy will come now.'"

Yancy looked up sharply.

"He said that?"

"He sure did. And the others laughed when he said it."

Yancy glanced at me and looked back at Bart.

"How 'bout that," Yancy said softly.

"What are you going to do?" Bart asked anxiously.

Yancy was quiet a moment.

Then he looked at Bart and said, "Tell Carlos we'll meet in front of the church in half an hour."

Bart's eyes grew wide.

"Half an hour? What if they leave?"

"They won't," Yancy replied. "Only reason they're here is to see me. Now go tell them."

"Yes, sir!" Bart said, and he wheeled around and left. However, instead of going toward the saloon, he headed up the street.

"Where you going?" Yancy yelled through the open window.

Bart slid to a stop.

"Fetching the undertaker," he explained. "I've got a dead man in my saloon."

"Oh," Yancy replied, then added, "You might mention he can be expecting more business *real* soon."

"Will do," Bart nodded and took off.

CHAPTER FORTY-NINE

Yancy and I finished our coffee, and the mood was somber as we thought on the task at hand.

"It's our fault," Yancy suddenly declared.

"What is?" I raised an eyebrow.

"Big Ben getting killed."

"How do you figure?" I asked.

"If we'd went down there earlier, Big Ben would still be alive."

I frowned as I thought on that.

"One way to look at it," I admitted, then added, "But we ain't the one who hit Emily, or have anger problems, or drink, or let our cows drift wherever they want."

"We don't even *have* a cow," Yancy lamented.

"Big Ben had it coming," I continued. "If not Carlos, somebody else would have killed him eventually."

"Tex, mebbe," Yancy reasoned.

"That's right," I agreed. "And, then we'd have to arrest *him*."

"We already did, once."

"And it wasn't pleasant," I reminded.

"You sorry Big Ben's dead?" Yancy looked at me.

"Not particularly," I admitted, then asked, "You?"

"Not so much."

"Be hard on Emily though," I reasoned.

"Might, for a while," Yancy replied, and then asked, "So, can you live with it?"

"Live with what?" I was confused.

"Live with knowing we're partly responsible," Yancy explained.

"I won't lose any sleep over it, if that's what you mean."

Yancy smiled briefly.

"Me neither," he said.

"So, what happens next?" I asked.

"We'll go down there and apprehend Carlos."

"He won't be apprehended peacefully," I warned.

"Don't imagine he will," Yancy agreed, then added, "We should tell the womenfolk. Emily and Little Ben need to be informed too."

"Yes, they should," my mood sobered at the thought.

"Will you do it?" Yancy asked.

I frowned and looked at him.

"What about you?"

Yancy gestured at the coffee stain in clear display on his shirt.

"I ain't getting married looking like *this*. I'll go get a new shirt and meet you back here."

I smiled wryly and shook my head.

"Fine," I grumbled.

Yancy smiled his appreciation, and we walked out into the street.

We started to split in different directions, but Yancy stopped abruptly. He tilted his head and frowned.

"You hear something?" He asked.

I did. Somebody was yelling, and the faint noise came from the direction of the jail.

Sheriff Wagons, I thought.

"Not if you don't," I replied.

Yancy looked thoughtful. He studied me, but my expressionless face revealed nothing.

"All right then," Yancy said after a moment, and he walked down the street.

I watched him go, and then I hurried toward our house.

CHAPTER FIFTY

I stepped up onto the porch at our house and walked in.

I was greeted with the sounds of girlish giggling, coming from the kitchen. It was a pleasant and welcome sound, and I couldn't help but smile.

Tussle, however, wasn't giggling. He was sitting in the front room, and he looked non-interested and bored.

Wyatt and Little Ben were also in the front room, playing a game of marbles on the floor. Their faces were flushed with excitement, and they hardly noticed me. I watched them a moment, and my smile turned into a grin.

"What are you doing here?" Tussle grunted, breaking the silence.

I looked at him.

"Did you hear the gunfire?" I asked.

"No. What gunfire?"

"Good," I said, and I walked toward the kitchen while Tussle scowled at me.

I paused at the doorway and looked in.

Jessica was in her wedding dress, and she looked beautiful. Josie and Emily were hustling all around her, and all three had red faces from laughing so much.

I hated to interrupt, and I stood there until Josie noticed me. I motioned at her, and she followed me back to the front room.

We went over to the corner, next to Tussle.

"You look good," she said as she studied me.

"That happens when I take a bath," I smiled at her. Then my smiled vanished, and I added, "We have a situation."

"Oh?"

Speaking softly so Little Ben wouldn't hear, I told her and Tussle what had happened. Concern filled Josie's face, and she bit her lower lip.

"You have to go down there?" She asked.

"I'm afraid so," I replied.

"Can't Sheriff Wagons handle it?"

"I'm afraid not."

"I don't like this," Josie pouted.

"Neither do I," I admitted.

"I'm going with you," Tussle declared.

I looked at him and frowned.

"I appreciate the offer, but no," I said.

"Why not?" Tussle scowled.

"Last time you tried to help, you almost shot your foot off with your own shotgun," I reminded.

"Aw, that was a long time ago," Tussle scoffed.

"Not really," I corrected, then added, "Besides, I'd feel better if somebody stayed here."

Tussle scowled at that. He glared at me and crossed his arms.

"Fine," he muttered. "I know when I'm not wanted."

Any reply would have only made Tussle madder, so I decided not to even try. Instead, I looked back at Josie.

"Emily and Little Ben need to be told about Big Ben," I hinted.

Josie understood, and she nodded.

"I will do it," she offered.

"Good girl."

"They will be sad, but it is for the best," Josie declared.

"My feelings exactly," I said.

"I will explain to Emily that this will lead to better things," Josie said.

"Good luck with that," I replied, then added, "Well, I gotta go."

"Coop," Josie said, her voice suddenly low and urgent.

"Yes?" I looked at her.

"Be careful."

I smiled reassuringly.

"See you at the wedding," I said.

CHAPTER FIFTY-ONE

Josie headed toward the kitchen. Tussle meanwhile, trying his best to look insulted, ignored me.

Wyatt and Little Ben were still playing marbles. I waited until they had finished their game, and then I cleared my throat.

"Wyatt," I said.

"Yes?" He looked up at me.

"We need to talk."

He noticed my somber expression and nodded. I walked outside, and he followed me out onto the porch.

"I need your help," I announced.

"Yes?" He asked curiously.

I explained all that had happened. Wyatt looked excited, and his eyes grew wide.

"I can shoot!" He exclaimed.

"Not that," I frowned. "Something else."

Disappointment showed in his face.

"You want me to stay here, with the womenfolk," he presumed.

"Yes, but I was talking about something else," I replied, then added, "It's about Tex."

"Oh?" Interest crept back into his face.

I paused while I gathered my thoughts.

"Tex isn't going to prison," I announced. "At least not for now."

Wyatt grinned with pleasure.

"You're giving him a chance?"

"Yancy and I are, yes."

"You won't regret it," Wyatt declared.

"We'll see."

"So what can I do?" He looked eager.

"Tex can't drink anymore," I explained. "It's part of the deal."

"Not even one drink?"

"Tex is an alcoholic," I replied. "He can't stop with just one."

Wyatt's expression sobered.

"That'll be hard for him."

"That's why he needs our help," I said. "All of us. I'm counting on you to keep an eye on him at the ranch."

"So you don't object, us working together?"

"I don't, long as he's not drinking."

"He won't," Wyatt declared. "I'll see to that!"

"Good boy," I said.

"While we have a moment, there's something else," Wyatt said abruptly.

"Yes?" I raised an eyebrow.

Wyatt shuffled his feet while he collected his thoughts.

"Tussle and I talked earlier," he said. "He offered me a full time job."

I thought on that and shrugged.

"You stay out there most the time anyway," I said.

"But this would mean me moving out to the ranch," Wyatt explained.

"Oh," I said.

My first impulse was to object, but then another thought intrigued me.

Since we'd been married, Josie and I had shared a house with someone. However, if Wyatt moved out, we would soon be all alone, just as soon as the Texas Ranger station was finished.

The more I thought on that, the more appealing it got, and I almost grinned.

"I could also keep a better eye on Tex," Wyatt spoke up, interrupting my thoughts.

I nodded slowly.

"Yes, you could at that," I said.

"So it's all right?" Wyatt looked excited.

"No objections here," I said. Wyatt grinned, and I added, "But let's break it to Josie *gently* this time."

"Yes, sir," Wyatt beamed.

I grinned briefly, but then my expression sobered as I looked down the street.

"Well, I gotta go," I said.

"Coop?" Wyatt replied.

"Yes?" I looked at him.

"Don't get shot."

"I'll try," I smiled.

"Are you scared?" He suddenly looked curious.

"Of what?" I asked.

"Dying."

I started to reply, but stopped when I recalled Wyatt's words from yesterday.

"I like to be scared," I jested. "It feels good."

Wyatt grinned and chuckled. I chuckled with him, and then I left the porch and walked down the street.

CHAPTER FIFTY-TWO

I walked through the open doorway of the Texas Ranger Station. Yancy was already there, and he was changing shirts.

"Nothing else had better happen," Yancy said when he spotted me. "This is the last shirt they have that fits."

"Best not drink anymore coffee then," I suggested.

Yancy frowned at me. However, before he could reply, Tex walked in behind me.

"I just heard Big Ben was killed," he announced.

I nodded and said, "Yes, we're on our way down there now."

"Does Emily know?"

"Josie's telling her."

Tex nodded, and he scratched his jaw as he stood there.

"I'm not sure how to feel about this," he admitted.

"I know; we feel the same way," I said.

"I'm sorry Big Ben's dead, but then again, I'm not either. Know what I mean?"

"More or less," I nodded.

"I also feel bad for Emily, but then I don't either. She'll be better off without him."

"She might not see it that way, at least for a while," I warned.

"She deserves better," Tex declared.

A thought suddenly occurred to me. It was an interesting concept, and I wondered if Yancy had already thought of it. It suddenly made sense, why Yancy had let Tex handle everything concerning Big Ben.

A smile crept over my face. Meanwhile, Yancy buttoned the front of his shirt and walked over to us.

"Have you thought anymore about our agreement?" Yancy asked Tex.

"It's *all* I've been thinking about," Tex admitted.

"Still believe you can do it?" Yancy asked.

"Not drink?" Tex asked.

"Yes."

"I'll do whatever it takes," Tex declared, then added, "I don't even *want* to drink. And I haven't felt that way in a long time."

"If you ever feel the urge, don't wrestle with it by yourself," Yancy instructed. "Tell somebody."

"I will," Tex declared.

"Good," Yancy said. He looked at me, and then added, "We forgot one small detail."

"What's that?"

Yancy puffed out his chest and tried to look important.

"As my Pa used to say," he drawled. "Any verbal agreement should end with a firm handshake."

A Texas-sized grin spread across Tex's face.

"I can do that," he said, and extended his hand.

Yancy grabbed it. Seconds later, his one good eye bulged slightly, and he uttered a surprised grunt as they exchanged a firm handshake.

Tex was enthused, and he squeezed especially hard. I heard a crunching sound, and Yancy's face turned red.

Tex finally released Yancy's hand, and he grinned and looked pleased. Meanwhile, Yancy dropped his hand to his side. He turned sideways so Tex couldn't see and shook his hand slightly.

I tried not to grin as I watched him.

CHAPTER FIFTY-THREE

While Yancy stood in the corner nursing his hand, I looked at Tex and cleared my throat.

"While we have a moment, I have something to say," I said, my voice stern.

"Yes, boss?" Tex look interested.

"It's about Wyatt," I announced.

A mixture of hope and fretfulness crossed his face while he waited for me to continue.

I paused a moment, and then explained about Wyatt's new job arrangement with Tussle.

"Good for Wyatt," Tex looked pleased.

"This means you two will be spending a lot of time together," I announced.

"We will?" He raised an eyebrow

"You will," I declared. "And, you're to teach Wyatt all you know about horses."

Tex grinned with pleasure.

"I can do that," he said, then asked, "Anything else?"

"Come to think of it, there is," Yancy spoke up from the corner.

We looked at Yancy. He was flexing his hand, and he looked thoughtful.

"Yes, boss?" Tex asked.

"Emily and Little Ben are spending the night at the hotel," Yancy informed. "I want *you* to escort them there after the wedding."

"I'd like that," Tex grinned.

"And tomorrow, I want you to take them home," Yancy instructed. "The ranch belongs to Emily now."

"Well, sure. I can do that."

"Emily's going to be lonely in the weeks to come," Yancy continued. "Whether she realizes it or not, she'll need some companionship. So, every Sunday morning, you are to go over there, pick them up in a buggy, and take them to church. It'll do Emily good to be around other folks."

Tex was startled.

"What if she won't go with me?"

"Just take a bath and shave. She'll say yes."

A faint smile crossed his lips.

"Yes, sir, boss."

"I also want you to help Emily with her cows," Yancy said. "That will also benefit Tussle."

Tex frowned as he pondered that.

"I'll have to ride over there almost every day," he mused. "Until it rains, those cows just won't stay put."

"Coop will talk with Tussle," Yancy replied. "I'm sure he won't mind."

"Neither will I," Tex grinned.

Yancy nodded.

"Well, that's about it then," he said.

Fearful of another handshake, Yancy slipped his hands in his pockets, as did I.

"I won't let you down," Tex said, enthused.

"I'm sure you won't," Yancy said, then added, "Well, we have to go."

"You want help?" Tex offered. "I ain't as good as you two, but I can shoot a coyote."

Yancy smiled briefly.

"We ain't going down there to shoot coyotes," he said.

"I'd still like to help."

"I appreciate the offer," Yancy replied. "But, it'd be best if you stayed out of it."

Tex nodded slowly, and he actually seemed relieved to be dismissed.

"I understand," he said.

"If something were to happen–," Yancy's voice trailed off.

"I'll look after the womenfolk," Tex vowed.

"'Preciate it," Yancy said.

Tex nodded. He looked at me, and then back at Yancy. Then he turned and left, and he walked with a newfound confidence.

CHAPTER FIFTY-FOUR

We checked our weapons.

Yancy wore his Colt revolver, and he had an extra one stuck in his waistband. As for me, I carried my rifle, and I also wore a Colt.

"You ready?" Yancy asked.

"Ready as I'm going to get," I replied.

Yancy nodded, and we went outside.

Side by side, we walked toward the church. Our movements were careful and precise, and our faces were without expression.

I felt calm, relaxed, and ready. From experience, I knew Yancy felt the same.

Like I always did before a gunfight, I tried to think of something else to talk about. It was always helpful, in an odd way, to have a distraction.

Sometimes, finding something to talk about was difficult. However, after the day we'd had, I had several subjects to pick from.

"How's the hand?" I asked, and grinned when I felt Yancy's glare.

"Just hope I can grip my Colt," Yancy complained, then asked, "Did Pa actually say that?"

"Nope. I just made it up," I chuckled, then added, "But, it sounds like something Pa would say."

"Does, don't it," Yancy agreed.

I nodded. It was quiet a moment, and I changed the subject.

"You've surprised me more than once today," I remarked.

"Oh?" Yancy prompted.

"I never took you as a matchmaker."

Yancy glanced sideways at me.

"Matchmaker?"

"Emily and Tex," I said.

"What about them?"

"You've been playing cupid all day," I accused.

Yancy grinned briefly.

"Ain't a bad idea."

"I like it," I replied.

"'Course, Emily will need some time to get over losing her husband," Yancy reasoned.

"No more bruises should help."

"And Tex ain't over losing his wife neither," Yancy continued.

"Sounded like Tex really loved her," I commented.

"He did," Yancy nodded. "And, he's still hurting. That's partly why I think they could help each other. They're both brokenhearted."

"Be interesting to see what happens," I remarked, then added, "I just hope we're alive to see it."

"We'll be fine," Yancy replied.

I nodded and squinted down the street.

"Well, they're waiting for us," I announced.

Yancy grunted.

Then he said, "I'll do the talking."

I was surprised, and I raised an eyebrow.

"Well, *this* is new," I commented.

"I'm gonna try to distract them," Yancy continued.

"Should work. You just distracted *me*," I replied.

"Just be ready to start shooting."

"I will be."

Yancy nodded, and we continued down the street.

CHAPTER FIFTY-FIVE

Carlos and his companions stood bunched together in the street, and behind them was the church. In an odd way, it looked sort of symbolic.

Carlos was watching Yancy, and a cruel, wolfish grin split his lips. He said something, and they spread out in a line and faced us.

We stopped in the street about thirty feet or so from them. Yancy's gun hand hovered naturally over his revolver's handle, and I held my rifle in the crook of my arm. I pulled the hammer back with my thumb, and it made a soft click.

We looked at them without expression, and they looked back. Not a word was spoken. A small whirlwind stirred up some dust between us, but we ignored the slight annoyance. Then the whirlwind disappeared and the dust settled.

Yancy finally cleared his throat. Then he smiled.

"You wanted to see me," he said, his voice dangerously soft.

Carlos narrowed his eyes.

"You killed my cousin," he accused.

"I did, but let's talk about something else," Yancy said abruptly.

Carlos blinked in surprise but didn't say anything.

"Wanted to thank you boys," Yancy continued. "That fella you killed has been giving us some trouble. Now we won't have to deal with him anymore. 'Course, I've got to lock you all up for a bit, but I'll speak to Judge Parker. We can probably work something out."

Carlos was obviously confused. He glanced at his companions and looked back at Yancy.

He started to reply, but Yancy interrupted him.

"Now, if you boys would kindly unbuckle your gun belts and follow me," he said.

Nobody moved. We just stared at each other, and the silence was thick with tension.

Carlos' eyes went hard and flat.

"No," he said.

Carlos was expecting more conversation, but Yancy was through talking.

"All right then," Yancy said, and in one smooth motion he palmed his Colt and fired.

There was a thumping sound, and Carlos jerked backwards as the bullet took him in the chest.

Even I was surprised by the suddenness of it, but I recovered quickly. I leaped forward, and in the same motion I leveled my rifle and pulled the trigger.

Everyone started shooting at the same time. I fired into the closest Mexican, and as he collapsed I worked the lever to my rifle and moved sideways.

There was a gasp beside me, and Yancy dropped to a knee. However, he still held his Colt, and he fired methodically into the Mexican next to Carlos.

There was only one still standing. I swung my rifle on him, and he fired right as I pulled the trigger.

There was a whistling sound as his bullet fanned air close to my head. At the same time, my bullet took him in the torso, and he cried out, grasped at his chest, and crumpled over.

I worked the lever again, and, holding it ready, surveyed the Mexicans. All four were down, and none were moving.

It was over.

I eased the hammer down on my rifle. Then I turned and looked at Yancy.

Now that the danger had passed, he dropped his Colt, grabbed at his arm, and let himself fall on his back. His face had a dull, pained look.

"Yancy?" I asked.

His voice was strained.

"Hit twice, I think," he said.

"Where?" I hurried over.

"Arm, and my leg."

"Well, that's a long ways from your heart," I replied as I looked him over.

I could see blood on his thigh, and another red stain was growing on Yancy's arm.

"We need to stop that bleeding," I said.

I took off my belt and vest. I rolled the vest up, knelt beside him, and made a clumsy pressure bandage on his thigh. Next, I studied his arm, but it wasn't bleeding as much.

"Should've waited to change shirts," I noted.

Yancy was in no mood to reply.

CHAPTER FIFTY-SIX

I heard running footsteps from behind.

I spun around with my rifle in hand, but then I spotted Josie. Wyatt, Dean, and Tex trailed behind her.

It must have been the threat of death, because my heart leaped with joy at the sight of Josie.

We looked at each other, and a relieved expression crossed her face. But then she glanced at Yancy, and the relief turned to concern.

"Yancy?" She asked.

"Don't worry; he'll live," I said.

"Are you sure?" She looked at him with uncertainty.

"He's been shot worse," I replied, then added, "I'll take him to the doc now."

"Jessica is worried," Josie looked at me. "She tried to follow me, but Tussle stopped her."

"Go tell her Yancy is all right," I replied.

Josie nodded, and then asked, "What about the wedding?"

"Get everyone to the church," I instructed. "We'll be there soon as Yancy quits bleeding."

"I'll tell Jessica," Josie said.

She turned and started back, but I stopped her as another thought occurred to me.

"How did Emily and Little Ben take the news about Big Ben?" I asked.

"They are sad, but they will be fine," Josie said.

I smiled, and so did Tex.

"Glad to hear that," I said.

Josie nodded. She smiled briefly at me, and then she and Wyatt headed back toward the house. Meanwhile, Tex and Dean came over to us.

"Need help getting Yancy to the doctor?" Tex offered.

"No," Yancy replied sourly before I could.

"I'd like to help," Tex replied.

"I can walk," Yancy scowled.

Tex wasn't so sure. He looked at me, and I shrugged.

"Don't mind Yancy," I said as I bent over, picked up his Colt, and stuck it in my waistband. "He's like this every time he gets shot."

Yancy glared at me, but I ignored the look. I reached down, grabbed Yancy underneath his arm, and pulled him to his feet.

Yancy grimaced in pain, hopped a bit, but managed to stay upright.

"You all right?" I asked.

"No," Yancy replied.

I nodded. I wrapped my arm around his midsection, and he leaned against me as we hobbled toward the doctor's office.

CHAPTER FIFTY-SEVEN

I always felt a little nauseous after a gunfight. While the doctor worked on Yancy, I sat in the corner and let the feeling pass.

Dean and Tex didn't stay long. Dean went to fetch the undertaker, and Tex went to our house to escort the ladies to the church.

Some color was returning to Yancy's face, and the shock of being shot was wearing off. However, he still displayed a sour expression.

"How is he?" I asked the doctor.

He was working over Yancy's thigh, and Yancy kept grimacing in pain.

"Got the bullet out," the doctor said without looking up. "It didn't hit anything too vital."

"And his arm?" I asked.

"Just a flesh wound. Bullet went clean through."

I grunted my satisfaction. I stood, walked over to the table, and peered down.

Yancy's arm was already wrapped and bandaged, and the doctor was in the process of bandaging his thigh.

"Gonna make it?" I asked Yancy.

"If I die, bury me with my coffee cup," he replied sarcastically.

I smiled and chuckled. Meanwhile, the doctor tied a knot in the bandage, looked it over, and grunted his approval.

"Come back in a day or two, and I'll change the bandage," he said.

"Thanks, doc," Yancy said, and he eased himself off the table.

"Can you walk?" I watched him.

"Not so well."

I spotted a crutch in the corner. I grabbed it and handed it to him.

"Here, stick this under your arm," I said.

He did, and he limped across the room.

"Good enough," I said, then added, "Let's go."

"Go where?" Yancy looked at me.

I scowled at him.

"Where do you think? The church."

"I can't get married like this," Yancy objected.

"Why not?" I narrowed my eyes.

"Look at my shirt," he gestured at the dark stain and tear on his sleeve.

"Jessica ain't marrying your shirt," I pointed out.

"But I look awful."

"Won't argue with that," I replied. "But, you're alive, and that's all that matters. Now come on, or I'll carry you there myself."

Yancy didn't look happy, but he still grabbed his hat and followed me to the door.

"Hold on," I said before we stepped out.

"What is it now?" Yancy glared at me.

"Making sure the street is clear," I replied.

Yancy didn't understand, and he looked at me oddly.

"It's customary for a bride not to see the groom before the wedding," I explained, and I stepped outside before Yancy could reply.

I looked down the street and spotted Tex. He was holding the church door open for all the ladies, and once they were inside he followed after them.

The undertaker was also down there, and he and his helper had just loaded Carlos and his companions into the back of a wagon.

I grunted my satisfaction and went back inside.

"Streets are clear, and Jessica is waiting at the church," I announced. "Let's go before something else happens."

Yancy looked somber. He took in a deep breath and nodded.

"Give me my Colt," he said.

I pulled the revolver from my waistband and handed it over.

He reloaded it, handled it some, and slid it in his holster. Then he looked at me and nodded.

"I'm ready," he said.

I returned the nod, and we went outside. Side by side, we moved down the street toward the church. Our pace was slow, and Yancy leaned heavily on his crutch.

Yancy looked nervous. I frowned at that, and then decided a distraction might help, just like before our gunfight.

"By the way," I said as we reached the church. "You owe me a new vest."

Yancy blinked in surprise. He frowned at me, but I opened the door to the church before he could reply.

"After you," I said.

We looked at each other a moment. Then, Yancy smiled and limped inside. I grinned, took my hat off, and followed after him.

EPILOGUE

The wedding went with no problems, although Yancy did have to sit while the vows were exchanged.

Afterwards, there was a joyous celebration, and even Tussle enjoyed himself.

After the festivities, Tex escorted Emily and Little Ben to the hotel. I watched from afar, and they seemed to enjoy each other's company.

I hung around the hotel lobby, fearful that Tex might feel the urge to go to a saloon. However, as soon as he said goodnight to Emily, he got another room in the hotel and turned in. Wyatt, determined to keep an eye on Tex, decided to bunk with him.

Josie and I were left alone after that, and our house was quiet and still as we walked in.

"I could get used to this," I told Josie, and she grinned in agreement.

It had been a long, stressful day. We undressed and crawled into bed, and I sighed in contentment as the silence soaked in.

A few minutes passed, and I was just about to fall asleep when a thought suddenly occurred to me. I gasped and sat up.

"Wagons!" I exclaimed.

"What?" Josie asked sleepily.

"I forgot all about Wagons!"

Josie didn't understand.

"Can't it wait until tomorrow?" She asked.

That was an interesting thought, and I scrunched my face as I mulled it over.

Then I grinned and said, "Reckon it can."

"Let's go back to sleep," Josie encouraged.

I squeezed Josie's arm in agreement, burrowed back under the covers, and allowed myself to relax. Seconds later, a satisfied grin crossed my face as I closed my eyes.

The End

Read the entire The Landon Saga series!

(Listed in order)
#1 Confessions of a Gunfighter
#2 Entwined Paths
#3 Cooper
#4 Rondo
#5 Yancy
#6 Lee
#7 They Rode Together
#8 Warpath
#9 Fastest Gun Around
#10 Midway

Also by Tell Cotten
Wanted: A Western Story Collection
(Includes THE MIRROR, a Landon Saga short story)
Wanted II: A Western Story Collection
(Includes THE MIRROR II, a Landon Saga short story)

Coming soon… book # 11 in The Landon Saga

Follow Tell Cotten on Bookbub! Simply click follow, and get an email with every new release.
https://www.bookbub.com/authors/tell-cotten

Want to connect to other fans of The Landon Saga? Join The Landon Saga fan group on Facebook:
https://www.facebook.com/groups/784798154926122/
Or you can like The Landon Saga Page on Facebook:
https://www.facebook.com/TheLandonSaga

About the Author

Born in West Texas, Tell Cotten is a seventh generation Texan. He comes from a family with a ranching heritage and is a member of the Sons of the Republic of Texas. Besides writing, he is also in the cattle business, and he resides in West Texas with his wife, Andi, and their two children.

Tell has enjoyed writing from an early age, and he also has a great love of the history of the west. MIDWAY is his tenth novel in The Landon Saga series.

For announcements of new releases and all other information, please like The Landon Saga Page on Facebook https://www.facebook.com/TheLandonSaga Or, you can join The Landon Saga Fan Group https://www.facebook.com/groups/784798154926122/ You can also visit Tell Cotten's website http://tellcotten.wordpress.com/

Acknowledgements

I would like to thank my wife and my family for all their help and support. Without them this wouldn't be possible. I'd also like to thank God for the gift of writing.

Special thanks goes out to Bill for the fantastic drawing, and thanks to Mike and Marcy for putting the cover together.

And lastly, I'd like to thank Melissa for all her advice, help, and hard work.

Have you read the rest of The Landon Saga? Enjoy this excerpt from book one, CONFESSIONS OF A GUNFIGHTER.

CONFESSIONS OF A GUNFIGHTER
Book one in The Landon Saga series

PROLOGUE

I had been shot. That I knew.

After that, it was just a guess. I didn't know how bad, or even where I'd been hit.

I had been unconscious for many days, and as I woke up, I was confused. I didn't know where I was or even what day it was.

I blinked my eyes as I looked up, and I was stunned to see metal bars all around me.

I was in a prison.

I was lying on a bunk, and my shoulder was bandaged.

I tried to move. It hurt, so I decided against it.

I was still lying there a while later when the outer door opened, and I heard boot heels walking up to my cell.

With pain everywhere, I sat up slowly and swung my feet out onto the floor.

"How you feeling?" I heard a voice say.

My mouth was dry and my tongue felt thick, so I swallowed and licked my lips.

"Horrible," I managed.

"You was shot."

"I know."

"Took us two days to find you. Rain came in, and we lost your tracks."

I looked up. At first everything seemed hazy, but then things slowly came into focus.

There were two men standing by my cell door.

One of them was a short, pudgy looking feller I'd never seen before. He wore a business suit and looked to be important.

The other person was Lieutenant Yancy Landon.

Every time I'd seen Yancy he'd been somber and serious, and when he spoke it was always clear, certain, and to the point.

He was a small man, much like myself. He was also real good with that Colt six-shooter of his.

"Well, cousin, looks like you've finally got me," I said.

"That is correct."

Suddenly I jumped, and the movement sent sharp pains throughout my body.

"The herd!" I exclaimed. "What happened to the herd?"

"Forget 'em. Those cows aren't your concern anymore," Yancy said.

I frowned.

"I was being paid to worry. It was my responsibility."

"It ain't anymore."

I was angry, but Yancy didn't seem to notice.

"I was going to turn myself in, soon as the cattle drive was over," I said.

"Sure. That's what they all say," Yancy replied.

"You didn't get my message?"

"I got it."

"I meant it, Yancy."

"Either way, doesn't really matter. I've got you now."

"So what do you want?" I asked irritably. "You ain't here to talk family history."

Yancy started pacing.

"I've been wanting you for a long time, cousin. Most all us Landons are known for our honesty and good will, but you're nothing more than a killer and a thief."

I was silent.

"But, bad as I've wanted you, there's another feller I've wanted even more."

I looked down at the floor and nodded slowly.

"I know," I said softly.

Yancy stopped pacing and turned to me.

"And, you're the only feller who knows where he is."

"How did you figure that?"

Yancy didn't reply. Instead, he turned and looked out the window, and his face was real thoughtful looking.

"I had a long talk with Lee Mattingly and Ross Stewart 'bout you."

"Oh?" I asked curiously. "What'd they say?"

"Plenty."

It was silent, and then Yancy turned and looked down at me.

"Rondo, these past few years I've heard all sorts of stories 'bout you."

"Seems I'm a favorite subject," I agreed.

"Not all those stories are true, are they?"

"Depends on which ones you've heard," I said.

"How 'bout the killing and the stealing?"

I was silent, and Yancy sighed and shook his head.

"I knew your Pa. He was a good and just man. How come you turned out so different?"

"It's a long story."

"We've got the time."

I looked up, surprised.

"You really want to hear it?"

Yancy glanced at the short, pudgy looking feller. He nodded, so Yancy turned back to me.

"We want to hear it."

"Why do you care?" I asked.

"We're interested," Yancy said, and he nodded towards his companion. "This here is Judge Parker. I want you to tell your story to him."

"Sorta like a confession?" I asked.

165

"Something like that."

I thought on that for a second.

"Why should I?" I asked.

"Clear your conscience for one thing," Yancy replied. "And, if you don't, then Judge Parker can personally guarantee you that you won't be seeing the sunshine again for a mighty long time."

Judge Parker nodded solemnly.

I exhaled loudly as I thought it over, and then I nodded. I had planned on doing this anyway, and I might as well get it over with.

"All right, I'll confess," I said.

"You've made a wise decision," Yancy said. "Need anything before you start?"

"Coffee'd be nice."

Yancy turned and left, and moments later he came back with a full coffee pot and three cups.

He poured the coffee, and he handed me a cup through the opening of the cell.

I cradled the cup with both hands, and I took a long swig and swallowed slowly.

"Good coffee," I said. "Tastes real sweet."

"It's got sugar in it," Yancy explained.

I took another swig while Yancy and Judge Parker pulled up some stools.

"I don't know where to start," I said.

"Beginning would be nice," Yancy suggested.

I thought for a moment.

"Reckon we'll have to go all the way back to my childhood then."

"Go ahead."

I collected my thoughts and started talking, and Judge Parker and Yancy listened closely.

CHAPTER ONE

Since I'm confessing, I'll go ahead and say that I've done some bad things. But, there's been a lot of lies told about me too. Gossip travels fast, and my name has sure gotten around.

Most folks say I'm an outlaw, a fast gun, and a killer. I have killed folks, but I never wanted or planned to. It's what life threw at me, and I had to deal with it accordingly. And, every feller I ever killed went down facing me.

As for me being a fast gun… that's true. I am mighty handy with a six-shooter, and my speed is right up there with the best. Course, I've had lots of practice over the years, so I should be fast after all that practicing.

It's also been said that I have a fierce temper, and I can't deny it. But, I think temper is the wrong word. Instead, it's more like a feeling that comes over me right before times of trouble.

It's a feeling that's hard to explain. The best way is to say that it's a feeling of confidence, calmness, loneliness, sharp keenness, and pure meanness all rolled up into one. It also dulls my senses, and many a time I had been hurt and didn't even know it until afterwards.

I'm not the only Landon that has experienced this feeling. It had happened with Pa, and Pa warned me often about it. But I wasn't worried, and I never gave it much thought until the day that it actually happened to me.

My childhood days were lived in eastern Louisiana. I was born on our small farm in 1851, ten years before the start of the Civil War. My Pa's name was Noley Landon, and Pa named me Rondo after a childhood friend of his.

Pa and me were always real close. In my eyes there was no better man, and I still feel that way.

My Ma got sick and died when I was a youngster, so I never did know her. But Pa talked of her often, and I know that he missed her.

My Ma had a younger brother named Elliot. He was only six years older than me, and my Ma took care of him growing up.

When my parents got married, Uncle Elliot sorta came with the arrangement. But Pa didn't mind, and Pa treated him like a son. As for me, Uncle Elliot was like a big brother.

Besides farming, we also bred and broke a few horses. Elliot preferred the farming end, but breaking broncs was my passion.

Pa was a real good hand with a horse, and he taught me all he knew. By the time I was fourteen, I was busting broncs and could ride just about anything. Pa said I was a natural, and my dream was to one day go out west and get a ranch job breaking broncs.

Looking back now, I reckon I can say that I had a normal childhood. Life was good, and I never was in much trouble. That is, until the day that I first experienced the feeling.

I was eight years old.

It was midmorning, and Pa sent Elliot and me to town to pick up some fencing supplies for the farm.

We were loading the supplies into the back of our buckboard when a local bully named Jake Bellows came walking up.

It was generally known that Jake was no good. His wealthy Pa owned numerous slaves, so Jake never had to work.

Jake and Elliot were always picking on each other, and I figured with no grown-ups near that trouble was coming fast.

On this particular morning Jake was extra cocky and full of himself. He was packing an old, rusty Colt pistol that his

Pa had just given him, and he was anxious to show it off. According to Jake, the corroded six-shooter still worked, and Jake claimed to be an excellent shot with it.

We went about our work, but Jake kept picking on Elliot about this or that.

Elliot finally had enough. He told Jake what he thought of him, and that made Jake fighting mad. Jake tossed the gun aside, and they started kicking, gouging, and fighting each other in the street.

Jake was a big, pudgy feller, and he was nearly twice the size that Elliot was. But that didn't bother ol' Elliot any, for Elliot was in good shape on account of all the hard work out on the farm.

They traded blows back and forth, and for a while it was an even match.

Jake's size finally started to break Elliot down. Elliot's face became a bloody pulp, but he was awful stubborn and wouldn't stop fighting.

The situation kept getting bloodier, and I was concerned that Elliot was about to get seriously hurt.

Suddenly I was mad, and that's when the feeling came washing over me. It made me lose control of myself, and before I knew it I was jumping into action.

I spotted Jake's Colt pistol lying on the ground, and I ran over and grabbed that six-shooter with both hands.

I didn't know it at the time, but by now folks down the street had spotted the fight, and they were running towards us to break it up. But I was sort of like in a fog, and could only see what was happening right in front of me.

"Hey!" I shouted. "That's my friend!"

And then, without any further warning, I pulled the trigger.

CHAPTER TWO

I didn't figure on hitting anybody. All I had wanted was to make some noise to break up the fight.

I fired four times, and folks dove for cover.

Finally, I couldn't make the six-shooter fire anymore, and somebody ran up and knocked the gun away from my grasp.

Jake was nowhere to be seen. But Elliot was thrashing around on the ground, yelling and grabbing at his foot.

As for the other shots fired, two of them were buried deep in our buckboard, and the other one knocked out a pane in the general store's window.

Pa had to pay for that window, and later on Pa made me pay for it back home behind the woodshed. It was the worst whipping I ever received from Pa, and thinking back on it now I can see how I deserved it.

Pa had a long talk with me that night, and he told me how bad I'd been. Pa was scared, and he told me sternly if I didn't learn to control my temper that I would wind up on the wrong side of the law someday.

I was real low after that, especially when I realized that I could have killed Elliot or someone else. At first Elliot was plenty mad, but after a while he warmed back up to me, saying he realized I was only trying to help, but that I just went about it the wrong way.

After that, I got the reputation as being no good. Whenever I was in town, folks would frown and shake their heads, and none of the youngsters my age would have anything to do with me. But I didn't care, because I liked being left alone.

Pa came and fetched me a few days after I shot Elliot in the foot.

"Judging by your shooting spread, I reckon I'd better show you how to work a gun proper like, or else you're liable to blow your own head off," Pa told me.

Pa was trying hard to look stern, but he couldn't help but reveal a small, amused smile.

Pa grabbed his rifle and took me out deep into the woods. He sat me down on a log, and then he showed me his rifle. Next, he showed me how to load it, and Pa made me load it in front of him while he watched carefully.

"Now then," Pa said as he stepped back. "Take aim at that branch over yonder."

I looked to where Pa was pointing, and the distance had to be at least seventy-five yards.

I took ahold of the rifle, and I squatted down behind the log and rested the barrel where I had just been sitting. I took a long, careful aim. Then, I let out my breath and squeezed the trigger.

The rifle boomed in my hands, and the branch exploded at the end.

Pa looked at me with a surprised look.

"Well now! That's pretty good shooting, son! Why, I think that's even better than I could do!"

I beamed with pleasure while Pa scratched his chin thoughtfully.

"Tell you what; you take some time everyday and practice, and then you and me will go out hunting. How does that sound?"

That sounded good, and I said so. Pa was true to his word, and a week later I killed a deer with Pa's rifle.

Pa and I went out a few more times, and then he started letting me do all the hunting by myself. I was good at it, and I hardly ever wasted any ammunition.

Pa bragged often that he had never seen a youngster be as good a shot as I was. Pa was proud, but he also made sure I understood that handling a gun was a very serious thing.

"A rifle is a tool," Pa told me sternly. "Sometimes you have to defend yourself with one, and that's not a bad thing. Just make sure you use a gun for the right reasons, and not the wrong ones. You kill the wrong man and it will haunt you for the rest of your life."

"Yes, Pa," I said.

Things went back to normal after the incident with Jake Bellows passed. Growing up on a farm would give any youngster plenty of excitement, and I treasured every minute of it.

I had no idea that it would someday all end. To a youngster things go on forever, but you find out real quick as you grow up that things change quickly.

I was ten years old. The year was 1861, and the Civil War broke out. Men from all over rushed off to war, and Pa was one of the first to go.

There's been some foolish talk that I avoided fighting in the war. Truth was, I wanted to go real bad.

My Pa was the youngest of three brothers by nine years, so I had a lot of older cousins that went and fought in the war. I reckon them going and me staying sort of made me look bad, but they were old enough and I wasn't, plain and simple.

Pa made Elliot stay behind too, for he said I was too young to stay by myself. Elliot was aggravated, but he finally gave in to Pa's wishes.

Pa instructed us to watch the place while he was gone, and we did just that. I helped Elliot with the farming, and when I needed help breaking one of the colts Elliot helped me. We both worked extremely hard, and when Pa came back the place looked even better than when he had left.

Pa came back home in 1863. Elliot and I were surprised, because the war was still on and we had received no word from Pa.

Pa told us that he had been shot and captured. He was then going to be sent up north to prison, but luckily he bumped into an older Yankee cousin of mine.

Turns out, it was Yancy.

Yancy helped Pa and a few others escape, and after that Pa hurried on back home.

Pa had been shot in the hip, and he never did make a full recovery. He was still in good shape and could do whatever he wanted, but he had to deal with a slight limp for the rest of his life.

Pa hadn't been back home much more than a week when I got the biggest surprise of my life. It was late in the day, and Pa and I were out behind the woodshed chopping up firewood when he asked me how old I was.

I stopped working while I silently added up the years.

"I reckon I'd be twelve, Pa," I finally replied.

"Well now, I figure that's old enough," Pa declared.

"Old enough for what?" I asked curiously.

"Stay here," Pa told me.

Pa sunk his ax blade into a log, and then he limped down to the house. He came back shortly, and he was carrying a fancy looking Colt six-shooter.

CHAPTER THREE

"I took this off a dead Union officer," Pa explained. "And, seeing how you have a way with guns, I thought you might like to have it."

I could barely contain my excitement as I reached out and took the six-shooter.

I don't know how, but as soon as my palm wrapped around the handle I knew I was going to be a natural. The six-shooter fit perfectly in my hand, and holding it was one of the most natural feelings I had ever felt before.

I gave the six-shooter a good going over.

The handle was made out of white ivory, and the short barrel was dark and polished. It had been well taken care of; there wasn't a scratch on it.

"I've never seen a gun any fancier than this," I said excitedly.

"Don't think I have neither," Pa agreed. "It's a well-built pistol, and I expect you to take good care of it. It should last you a lifetime."

"I'll take good care of it, Pa," I reassured him. "I surely will!"

From that moment on, that Colt and me became inseparable. It didn't matter what I was doing; I always wore it, and I practiced with it every chance I had.

But spare time was hard to come by.

Running a farm was hard work. There was always something to be done, and it seemed like there was never enough daylight.

Hard life as it was, to me it was still a mighty good life, and I never wanted it to end. But, as usual, things changed.

Two years later, the war finally came to an end.

Pa thought things would get better, but he was wrong. Reconstruction people from the North started moving in, and they took away property and gave everybody that fought for the South fits.

We all stayed away from town during that time, and Pa kept his rifle handy. But then came the night that they came out to the farm.

We had just finished supper when we heard a noise. I looked out the window and spotted them.

There was a buggy in front, and in it was an important looking businessman. Behind the buggy trailed about twenty Yankee soldiers riding a-horseback.

Pa's face got hard and dark, and he told us sternly to stay inside. Pa grabbed his rifle, and he opened the door and walked out to meet them.

The man in the buggy pulled up in front of Pa. They talked in low, sharp tones while Elliot and I pressed up against our window and watched.

They didn't talk for long.

Pa turned away abruptly. He walked back to the house while the buggy and the soldiers turned and left.

Pa walked inside, shut the door, and sat down heavily at the table while Elliot and I watched curiously. Pa stared blankly at the floor, but he finally looked up at us.

"Well, boys," Pa told us, "Those Reconstructionalists say we owe 'em a lot of money in back taxes, and if we don't pay they'll confiscate the farm."

"What does 'confiscate' mean, Pa?" I asked.

"It means they'll take our farm away from us," Pa explained. "It isn't right, but there's nothing we can do about it. The law's on their side, not ours."

"I know something we can do!" Elliot blurted angrily. "We've got guns, ain't we?"

"Son, there's no use fighting it," Pa said with a weak smile. "If we did they'd just send more Yankee soldiers, and we can't fight 'em all."

"Can't we come up with enough money?" I asked hopefully.

Pa shook his head.

"Not in this lifetime."

"Then what'll we do?" I wanted to know.

"I had a feeling this would happen, and I've been giving it some thought for some time now," Pa said with a touch of hope in his voice. "With things the way they are now, we can't go north, and if we stayed here in the south we would just be pestered more by those Northerners. And I don't think I could stand too much more pestering."

"So what *can* we do?" I asked, confused.

"We'll go west," Pa declared.

CHAPTER FOUR

"I met an old cattleman named J.T. Tussle during the war," Pa explained. "We were both prisoners, and to pass the time we talked some. I told him about our little farm, and Tussle told me all about his big cow operation he has out in West Texas near a little cow-town called Midway.

"We got to know each other pretty good, and before we split up he offered me a job if'n I wanted one. But I told him no, 'cause I had to get back here. He understood, but he said if things didn't work out to look him up, and the job would still be there. So, I figure that's what we'll do, boys. We'll get ourselves an outfit put together and head west."

That was good news as far as I was concerned. Going west was what I had always dreamed about, and I was eager to get started.

Those Reconstructionist folks must have been just as eager, because Pa said we needed to be gone within a week.

We started getting ready to leave the next morning.

The first thing we did was to help Pa load up some of the farming equipment into the back of our buckboard. Then, Pa went over to the corrals and cut out all but three of our riding horses to be sold.

I wasn't happy about that, but Pa said we had no choice. We needed a wagon, and those horses would bring a good price.

Pa left Elliot and me a long list of chores, and then he took off to town in the buckboard, leading behind him the long string of horses.

We worked hard all day, and Pa didn't make it back until almost dark.

Pa was riding in a brand new Conestoga wagon, and he also had a brand new team of horses pulling it.

As soon as we saw Pa, we dropped what we were doing and ran over to have a look.

The wagon was sparkling clean and had a crisp, white canvas tarp on top. It was sixteen feet long and also had a false bottom to hide valuables in.

Elliot and I climbed all over that new wagon, and then I looked over the new team of horses.

They were a fine-looking team. They were young, big boned, stout looking, and real gentle.

We also still had the three horses that Pa had decided to keep. But they were for riding purposes only, and unless one of the team got crippled or hurt they wouldn't be used to pull the wagon.

Pa had already explained that Elliot and I were going to ride a-horseback to save the team from pulling the extra weight, and that suited me just fine. I would rather be a-horseback any day than have to ride in a wagon, new or not.

***

We left early one morning. Pa's face was hard and stern when he woke us, and we were in somber moods as we got dressed.

After breakfast, we helped Pa hitch up the wagon. Then, while Pa checked over everything, Elliot and I saddled our horses.

I rode a little sorrel horse named Slim that was considered mine.

"You boys ready?" Pa asked as he climbed up onto the wagon seat.

We nodded, so Pa clucked at the horses.

It was hard riding away for the last time.

I reckon it was the hardest on Pa, and I'm sure he felt like he was leaving part of himself behind.

As for me, I had a big lump in my throat, and I didn't dare look at Pa or Elliot for fear that I would break out and cry.

We walked our horses towards the end of the lane. When we got there I pulled up Slim and looked back, but I was the only one.

Pa and Elliot kept going forward steadily, so I turned toward them and kicked up Slim, and we put the farm behind us for good.

__Want to keep reading? The Landon Saga is available here:__
https://www.amazon.com/Confessions-Gunfighter-Landon-Saga-Book-ebook/dp/B00A9L3GUQ/ref=la_B00BTNWC4Y_1_11?s=books&ie=UTF8&qid=1492214552&sr=1-11

www.ingramcontent.com/pod-product-compliance
Lightning Source LLC
Chambersburg PA
CBHW060945180626
46817CB00004B/1718